I0730123

SANCTUARY THIRTEEN

Copyright © 2025 Paul F. Horvitz All rights reserved.

This is a work of fiction. Any resemblance of a character to actual persons, living or dead, is coincidental, though it may seem like history's way of saying "I told you so."

No part of this book may be reproduced, or stored in a retrieval system, or transmitted in any form or by any means, electronic, mechanical, photocopying, recording, or otherwise, without the written permission of the author.

ISBN 978-1-7371519-2-0

SANCTUARY THIRTEEN

A Novel

PAUL HORVITZ

For my grandchildren, and in homage to George Orwell

~

Books by Paul Horvitz

Agent of Intrusion

The Tinker's Son

"I'm taking the future. It belongs to me."

— *The Eternal Quotations of Acton Grudge*

1

The front-door buzzer echoed through the house in three sharp bursts, interrupting a ritual that Dash Askin had always prized. He was brewing America Numero Uno dark roast coffee, which helped ease the gauzy nothingness he felt most mornings in the era of Bossism. Upstairs, Polly, the woman with whom he commiserated and shared a bed, was herding their daughter to breakfast. The spaniel Winston, never a barker, induced a full-body stretch on the inside doormat after the buzzer roused him from a blissful sleep.

Dashiel Nathan Askin — father, husband, software scientist, and bona fide Enemy of the People — brushed the errant coffee grounds from his hands and glanced through the narrow window that flanked the front door. Three wide-body Enforcers stood in navy blue uniforms with gold epaulets and the reassuring command "Law and Order" emblazoned on their chests.

Dash let out a sigh and called through the door with the indifference of a postal clerk, "Am I being arrested?"

"We got a warrant, Mr. Askin. Can you open up?"

Dash gripped the knob for a long moment. When he finally cracked the door, the early heat of the day floated into his face through the tight ranks of the Enforcers, each wearing a 9mm Smith & Wesson nestled in a black leather holster. They smiled in unison, and Dash had the instant and bewildering impression that the cops were ending a beat assignment with gratification rather than beginning one with apprehension. Their small yellow breast patches bore insignias that told Dash all he needed to know. He suppressed the thumping of his heart, willed himself into a state of outer calm, and told himself: "Just do what you always said you'd do."

Opening the door wider, Dash grumbled, "Law and Order at 7 a.m.? I haven't even had my coffee."

The Enforcer in the middle pushed a wide smile out to the edges of his cheeks.

"As we like to say in the Cleansing Squad, you get 'All the Law and Order you Deserve.' Thanks for opening up, Dashiel."

"I use Dash."

"Well, then I'll call you Dash. Just wanna be friendly. It's easier. What kind of a name is Askin, by the way? I've heard that name somewhere. It rings a bell." The Enforcer winked.

Dash felt testy but maintained a deliberate tone as his six-foot frame clenched. "Can we get to the point here?"

"Yes, sir, Mr. Askin. I mean Dash," the Enforcer continued. "Like I said, we're with the Cleansing Squad and we do have some complaints from your colleagues and neighbors that you're showing major signs of Derangement. You know, defaming The Boss. Disparaging Bossism. Telling your kids things about The Boss that might set them on the wrong path. So that's what we need to discuss."

"Dash? What's going on?"

It was Polly, the person Dash trusted most in a world where trust was a speculative bet if not a vice.

"One second, hun."

If Dash and Polly had been alone, he would have held both her hands, looked her in the eyes, and told her calmly, "It's what I've been warning you about since we met," as if he were asking her to waltz with him into a bomb shelter.

The officer leaned low around Dash's waist and flashed a jumbo grin. "Yes, ma'am, we do have a warrant for your husband's arrest, so if you could just step back a bit. We do need to process this situation today."

"Dash?" Polly pleaded. She folded her arms across her chest and didn't move.

Dash feigned weary exasperation, looked straight at the Enforcers, and asked, "You're charging me with Deranged Lunacy, aren't you."

"Well, DL is the infraction, yes sir."

The charge of Deranged Lunacy was a good sign, Dash figured. The Enforcers seemed clueless about the depth of his Boss Hatred. If they had figured out he was a hard-core subversive, or what the regime labeled a "domestic terrorist," he surely would have faced a masked assault unit of the Boss Bureau of Investigation armed with automatics and bearing a fresh sedition warrant. The more they think I've developed a garden-variety case of Deranged Lunacy, the better, he thought.

Dash smirked, wrinkling his close-cropped beard of dark browns and streaks of gray.

"I guess you think I'm one of those people who refuses to fly the Boss Nation flag," he said, "or obey The Boss's ludicrous 'Making Things POSSible' slogan."

The officer shook his head like a disappointed father. "You're not really *with* The Boss, are you, Dash, I mean, not even neutral. More like a textbook Enemy of the People, right? POSS is just a concept to believe in, son, but you don't believe in it, do you. You don't care about Prayer, Order, Security, and Shut-up-ism, but that's the glue that holds us together. You've gotten it into your head that you're right and everyone else in this community is wrong. Think about it. You might've lost touch with reality. That's what we're checking on. Derangement."

"I'm not answering any questions," Dash responded icily.

"He's not answering questions," echoed Polly with a tone of finality.

"Now, missus, please step back."

Polly was barefoot in jeans and a beige blouse that she hadn't had time to tuck in. She stood her ground. The chief Enforcer turned back to Dash.

"So what we propose to do, Dash, is to hold a hearing right here in your home. Judge McConicle, the Sanity Arbiter, is on his way. You know, gather the facts and reach a conclusion beyond a reasonable doubt. You'll have your say, of course. It's all fair. Very American. He should be here any minute. Then we can get started. Do you mind if we come in? It's awful hot out."

"You said you had a warrant," Dash said firmly, arms folded on his chest. "I need to see it."

"In due time, Dash. In due time. No need to raise your voice."

Dash didn't think he'd raised his voice, though it was insistent and firm.

"What is the *evidence?*" he demanded. "I know exactly what reality is, Officer. I've never lost touch." Inside his gut, the itch of angry rebelliousness was strong. "Did you ever consider the possibility, sir, that it's The Boss who's deranged? I want you to be the first to know that I have *never, ever* called The Boss a derelict, or an idiot, or an egomaniac, or a paragon of corruption, or even a nasty little shit. I have *never* done that. I'm not in *that* class of fools!"

"Hold on now. You're gonna have to practice some serious Shut-up-ism once Judge McConicle gets here. I'm not sure what a pentagon of corruption is, but everything else you just denied sayin,' which you're actually sayin', would land you in jail if you'd said 'em, which you just did. I'm not stupid, Mr. Askin. I know what you're up to, and I even know who raised you — with the help of the *Red* Chinese, isn't that right? But I'll let that little detail go for now. We're just doin' our job. It's up to the judge to decide if you've crossed the line and need to be declared a DL. Our job is to investigate every report of Deranged Lunacy before you people can do more damage."

The Enforcer paused. "Hey, I'm just wondering, Dash, are you a Christian?"

"No!" Polly blurted with the speed of a game-show contestant.

"Well, sort of," Dash lied.

"Sort of?" queried the officer.

"Why wouldn't I like a good guy like Jesus Christ? He's not on my Enemies List."

"Well, that's good. Glad to hear it. We all got our Enemies Lists, but you know, we don't hate the DLs. We really don't. We pity 'em. Deranged Lunatics have lost touch with reality, that's all. They let their anger overwhelm them. Do you think the DLs are facing reality, Dash? I mean, clearly they're not. And from what we're hearing, you're leaning pretty far into that Derangement camp. But like I say, it's up to the judge."

"Who the hell is telling you I'm Deranged? It's bullshit. I have a right to know who's informing on me, saying *crazy* things like I think The Boss is a power-mad despot and a bloodthirsty mafioso."

"Just take it easy, Dash. Like I said, we gotta wait for the judge. That's my orders, and that's what we're gonna do. So cool the foamin' jets."

"Jesus!" Dash exclaimed softly, grabbing a shock of brown hair at his forehead and thrusting it back with his fingers. He shook his head in frustration and fought to keep himself from emitting a more egregious profanity. "I mean, Jesus help me!"

Part of him meant it, too, though he knew it was odd for a Jew to invoke any member of the Holy Trinity. Dash understood exactly where this Derangement investigation was leading. He'd trained his mind for the day he'd be cuffed and taken away. That's what he'd told Polly for so many years with complete conviction. This was surely the day. He wanted to keep his chin high and do it right, and he knew Polly would be at his side, fearless to the end. It was Lily he worried about.

Dash turned his back to the Enforcers and looked for his daughter. Lily was sitting on the stairs, beautiful in her pigtails and unicorn pajamas, but looking as if she'd just witnessed a dump truck run over a kitten. Polly, who had retreated to be with her, was on the carpet at the base of the stairs, stroking Winston's floppy ears and quietly singing "Amazing Grace" the way a hymn ought to be sung.

Everett McConicle was raised on a family farm in central Indiana with six siblings who helped harvest the rotating crops of corn and soybeans. It was a devout household, and when he went off to college, Everett decided to major in Christian Law. He was among those who believed the country had lost its way some decades before and needed to remain vigilant to retain the primacy of the Law of the Bible. And that's why The Boss picked McConicle for the coveted and well-compensated position of Sanity Arbiter.

McConicle was only in his forties when The Boss created the role of Arbiter. It was a heady time. Under The Boss's newly centralized rule, he had determined that The Party was no longer needed and ordered it to close its doors. Most of The Party's propaganda responsibilities were shifted to a new grassroots organization, The League of Christian Voters, which The Boss seeded with ex-Party toadies and funded through universal payroll deductions. The Boss purged the army of non-believers and instituted a set of five-year plans for managing the Bosseconomy. At the same time, he launched The Great Cleansing, a crusade that went beyond previous campaigns to rid the nation of non-White migrants. The new aim, The Boss said, was to "find and rehabilitate anyone who doesn't fit in the New America." If you weren't like The Boss or just didn't like him, you didn't fit. He said it was all part of "the Second American Revolution." The Boss was a flawless purveyor of fear, and most people seemed to take it in stride, either because sadism appealed to them or they were terrified. He even let it be known that he kept two biographies of Joseph Stalin at his bedside, as if one was not enough to convey his message of intimidation.

Everett McConicle's sanity decisions placed him on the front lines when The Great Cleansing pivoted to anti-dissident work. The Boss's Chief Cleansing Officer oversaw all the Arbiters, who worked for a quasi-judicial unit called the Mind Disorders Bureau. They were like magistrates for malcontents. The system was flawlessly efficient, organized and monitored via the Universal Crosscheck Database. Helpful citizens called in tips to the Participation Hotline. Cleansing Squad Enforcers ferreted out people who couldn't bring themselves to worship The Boss. Then, Arbiters dispatched most of the apostates to a network of guarded campuses called Sanctuaries, where the goal was to rid the disgruntled of mind disorders like Deranged Lunacy.

McConicle was seventy-six and still processing subversives and resisters, albeit at a less frenetic pace, when he brought his mobile Cleansing operation to the Askin residence. It wasn't less frenetic because McConicle was no longer up to it but because most subversives, tens of thousands of them, had already been identified and neutralized.

The judge steered his baby blue snub-nosed pickup truck to the curb in front of Dash and Polly's house just as Dash uttered "Jesus help me!" Another man exited the passenger seat, a short fellow wearing thick, black-rimmed glasses that overwhelmed his face. He seemed to be swatting bugs around his face even though it was October — a warm one, to be sure — and the no-see-ums had already gone underground.

McConicle was rail thin, mostly bald, and had trouble standing fully erect. But he smiled easily and spoke with a kind tone. In his billowy black robe, a size too big, McConicle looked like a church choirmaster in a weight-reduction ad.

"Morning, officer. Morning everyone," the judge said cheerily as he and the swatter made their way up the brick walkway to Dash's front door. McConicle rolled a small suitcase behind him. To no one in particular, he announced: "This is Dr. Stancil. Ready to get started?"

Dash didn't move. "Judge, I demand to see the evidence."

McConicle's mien deflated, his smile replaced by a quizzical scowl. "You will have all the evidence, sir, once we start. I can assure you of that. Now please stand aside or I'll have these Enforcers restrain you. They have the equipment to do it. And I don't think you want your family to see that, now do you? Besides, it's a lot cooler inside."

Dash relented and strode into the dining room. There was no point in making a scene outside of the official hearing about to unfold. Polly and Lily sat together on the stairs in the center hall, staring.

"Dash?" said Polly, not plaintively but more in the vein of "Do your best; I love you."

"Dad?" said Lily, alarm written all over her twelve-year-old face.

"Bring Lily down here, hun," Dash said. "She needs to see what a kangaroo court looks like." Lily knew that court was for people who'd done something wrong, but she wondered why it was called "kangaroo."

"Alright, now," McConicle admonished. The judge silently pointed to a dining room chair opposite him and kept his crooked finger in the air until Dash sat, folded his hands together, and willed himself to keep his roiling emotions in check. Polly made her way into the room and stood with her arms wrapped around Lily, who felt a sudden chill from the air conditioning system groaning in the background. The three Enforcers sat down, flanking a seat intended for Judge McConicle. Dr. Stancil, still swatting something with his left hand, took a seat off to the side and placed a briefcase on his lap. The judge opened his suitcase and set up a tripod and video camera so deftly you knew he'd done it hundreds of times before. He sat and opened a thick spiral notebook, motioning Polly to turn on the chandelier's bulbs. Lily began whimpering in tiny squeaks.

"So, ladies and gentlemen, the camera's on," McConicle said, speaking professorially. He cleared his throat and noted the date, time, and place.

"I am Everett McConicle, a duly appointed Sanity Arbiter, and this is Derangement Hearing H-7492. These proceedings are authorized under USC Title Fifty-Eight. We're gonna record this hearing for any approved party to see. Nothing secret here. All open and aboveboard. My job is to determine whether the defendant is so deranged and out of touch with reality or so belligerent as to be a threat to himself or others. If determined at this hearing that he is Deranged, I have the authority to dispatch him to an institutional setting where he'd be unlikely to hurt others, and if he did hurt himself, well, that'd be a shame but we did our best to avoid it."

Dash was alternately frowning and smirking.

"Let us pray," said McConicle, bowing his head. "Lord, grant us the Strength and Wisdom to see Your Truth. In Jesus's name, we pray. Blessed Be The Boss. Amen." He looked up and smiled at Dash. "I'd advise you to remain in Shut-up mode until spoken to, Mr. Askin. Just answer the questions truthfully. We'll get to the evidence, I promise. If you object rudely or make ill-mannered faces, it will only be evidence of Derangement and noted in the record. Let's begin with the oath."

The judge turned to Stancil, who produced from his briefcase a leather-bound, gold-embossed American New Testament Bible with a Foreword by The Boss. He returned to his seat and kept swatting. McConicle slid the book across the table.

"Please place your hand on the Bible and repeat after me: 'I, Dashiel...'"

"I'm protesting this hearing," Dash interrupted matter-of-factly.

"Duly noted, Mr. Askin. Nonetheless, let's have the oath." A hint of exasperation colored McConicle's voice.

"I will not be taking an oath, Judge, and certainly not on *that* Bible. You'll just have to believe me or not." Dash thought of his late father and how pleased he'd have been to witness his son's implacability.

"I'd urge you not to detach yourself from reality any further, Mr. Askin. But we can go forward, if you insist. Your protest is noted. We don't bother converting hard-core atheists or Jews. Waste of time. Please state your name."

Head high, Dash spoke every syllable of his name as if in a dream that scrolled through his entire life in seconds. "Dashiel...Nathan...Askin." He felt at peace, even relaxed, now that the hearing had begun.

"And please state your age, marital status, occupation, and place of employment."

"Forty-three years old. Married to Polly. I do research on Autonomic Intelligence at CompuLink Machines International."

A female Enforcer leaned over and whispered something to the judge.

"Right, so now, Mr. Askin, I'm going to hand you the warrant for your inspection. I believe you requested that."

The Enforcer gave McConicle a single folded piece of paper, and the judge pushed it across the table.

"While you look that over, we're gonna proceed," McConicle said. "Even though I think I know the answer, I need to ask for our records. Mr. Askin, have you accepted Jesus Christ in your heart?"

Dash smirked. "Did you forget, judge, that I'm Jewish? So was Jesus, by the way. Probably one of the most humane and humble Jews of all time. I believe in the Grace of Nature and Humanity, Your Honor. But if you're asking if I like Jesus, the answer is, sure. Love the man. Exceptional human."

"Well, you seem to have forgotten about the Virgin Birth, Mr. Askin. I am asking if you accept Jesus as *Your Savior*, regardless of your religious preference, that's all. Because it would help your case. Plenty of Jews have accepted Jesus Christ, you know. Some of them are good friends of mine."

"It doesn't appear, Judge, that anyone real or mythical is swooping in here to be my savior. I'm obviously beyond saving. But as I said, I do think highly of Jesus of Nazareth. A damned good carpenter, I hear."

"Okay, then. We don't discriminate, Mr. Askin. I just need to know for the Universal Crosscheck Database. There are plenty of believers in Jew-day-ism, by the way, who've chosen to be members of the League of Christian Voters. I believe most of them belong to the Conformative wing of your religion. The League's open to all faiths, as you know, especially those who acknowledge the supremacy of Christianity in this world. But you're not a member of the League, are you, Mr. Askin?"

"Must have been an oversight," Dash lied.

"Yes, I'm sure it was an oversight. You do pay League dues, though. We have the Contribution records."

"It comes out of my paycheck, so I don't have a choice, do I."

"Everyone needs to be community minded in the Land of the Free and the Home of the Brave, Mr. Askin, and this is one of the Required Discretionary Contributions. Now, do you have any religious or spiritual tattoos?"

"I do not."

"Are you against tattoos, Mr. Askin?"

"Nobody will give me one that says: 'Jesus Was a Jew.'"

"Now, that's the kind of smart-aleck answer that indicates Derangement, Mr. Askin. I hope you understand that. It will be noted in the record. But let's move on. Have you ever set foot in Pacifica?"

"No, never." This was the truth. Though Dash could have slipped over the border before the wall went up, he chose to remain. Giving up wasn't in him, and being a Boss Dodger just didn't feel right.

"You don't have a passport, do you?" the judge asked.

"Not anymore, thanks to you fascist folks." Dash smiled.

"Oh my, my, Mr. Askin. Do you think that word hurts me? No, sir. It hurts only you. Think about that the next time you're inclined to blurt out these meaningless labels. Think hard. It hurts only one person, and that's you. Let's move on. Now, in examining the digital contents of your phone, which the BBI has done remotely under a court order, we detected the same unusual message about a dozen times in the last six months. This message was sent to various people in your contacts. I'm referring to the message that says, 'The elephant dances at dawn.'"

McConicle stopped and stared at Dash, who stared back until the judge relented.

"Why don't you tell me what that means, Mr. Askin, 'The elephant dances at dawn.' It's obvious that's code for something. You need to tell the truth, son. This would be a good time to start. It'll help your case."

Dash failed to contain the grin that crept halfway across his face. "With respect, Judge McConicle, I'm not your son. And the phrase you detected so intrusively, without my authorization, is a benign cultural reference to Hannibal's defeat of the Romans. Completely harmless. It was around the time of Jesus, I believe, give or take a couple hundred years. Anyway, it's not a message at all. I use the phrase to remind friends I correspond with that strength and grace live side by side, in harmony. It's a gesture of encouragement. Get it? Dancing elephants. I'm sure you see that, Judge McConicle, being a man of..."

The judge interrupted. "What I know is you're too clever for your own britches, Mr. Askin, and I do believe you're hiding something. You *are* hiding something, aren't you."

"No, sir," Dash lied.

"These rambling excuses for answers will weigh against you, Mr. Askin. Your nonsense will be a noose you've fixed right around your own neck. But we can move on. I have another hearing scheduled. Now, I see from our investigative file that you used encrypted messaging until it was banned. Isn't that correct?"

"You are correct, Judge. There was nothing illegal about it when it was legal, now was there."

"True. We're merely establishing the facts. Confirming our data. Not everybody used encryption, but I note that you chose to be an Encryptor."

"I have to say, Judge, it does sound evil."

"Never mind. Ever had Halcitol injections, Mr. Askin?"

"Never."

"Really? You don't like Halcitol? It's a miracle drug, you know."

"I like a clear head. If you'll pardon the expression, Fucked-Up-ness doesn't really suit me."

"Alright. Noted. I see you don't fly the Boss Nation flag beside the Broad Stripes and Bright Stars on your front lawn. It's not yet a Required Discretionary, but most people do, you know. I expect someday soon it will be a Required Discretionary. Why don't you fly the flag, Mr. Askin? You don't like it?"

"That'd be putting it mildly. It symbolizes collective intimidation. You might as well ask why I don't take opiates. No, thank you." Dash liked that answer and thought his late father would have liked it, too.

As soon as he finished answering, a chorus of shouts arose from out on the street. Through the window behind the judge, Dash could see a group of people holding signs, but he couldn't read them. Then the shouts grew louder. They were angry and rhythmic.

"De-Range-Ment! De-Range-Ment! De-Range-Ment!!"

It was plain for everyone in the house to hear. Polly drew Lily close so that one ear was pressed into her mother's side and the other covered by Polly's hand. But Lily could hear it, and it made her want to run back upstairs and climb under her covers with Winston. She gritted her teeth and stood still.

Dash muttered, "What an honor…"

"What's that, Mr. Askin?"

"Nothing, Judge. I'm just enjoying the recital."

"Well, never mind. I have to say that's a strange answer to the flag question. Do you fancy yourself a *Marxist*, Mr. Askin?"

"A Marxist? As in Karl?"

"Communists are atheists, you know, and atheism is un-American."

"So I've heard."

"Now, do you have any books here in the house by Vera Hopkins?"

"Never heard of her," Dash lied. "Maybe her books were part of the first Big Burn, or the second? I don't know. That was a while ago. I was a kid."

"What about Ansel Williams, Phil Birnbaum, or Sarah McVeigh. Do you own any books by those so-called writers?"

"I've never heard of them, either," Dash lied again. "Look around, Judge. See whatever you want. Check the shelves. I've got a wonderful Popular Mechanics book called *The Down and Dirty of Toilet Repair,* and I have to confess that I secretly love Boss Housekeeping's *Seventy-Five Ways to Make Delicious Hamburgers.* That's mostly what we have. Some National Geographics. Oh, we do have a little poetry. The usual Frost. But I'm sure none of them are banned — well, unless you've banned that gay Chinese poet. I've forgotten the name."

"Chinese, did you say? Well, probably. And that other word is banned, you know. You should know better than to use a banned word in front of a Sanity Arbiter, Mr. Askin, let along your own child. And poetry? Always risky. That book has three strikes. Banned, banned, and banned. Better go ahead and hand it over."

Dash turned in his chair. "Can you get it, Polly?" He looked back at the judge. "I guess the Power & Light

Company is holding a poetry slam to keep the boilers fired up, right?"

"I was wondering the same thing," Polly interjected. She smiled at Lily, who smiled back and whispered "me, too" even though she didn't know what a poetry slam was. Dash turned and winked at both of them. He felt better.

"Alright, that's enough from both of you," McConicle said sternly. "It's only hurting your case, Mr. Askin. Keep digging that hole for yourself. We're moving on to the evidence now, since you were so eager to do so. Officer Eckholm, would you please read the affidavit from Mr. J.B. Carouthers. You know J.B. Carouthers, Mr. Askin?"

"Yep. He lives in the neighborhood."

"Mommy!" Lily exclaimed, realizing she goes to school with J.B.'s son, Tony. Polly shushed her.

The Enforcer named Eckholm thrust his shoulders back so the words "Law and Order" unwrinkled and inflated on his chest. "I interviewed Mr. J.B. Carouthers on September seventeenth at his home. He said, quote, 'We were walking our dogs. I asked Mr. Askin if he had heard The Boss was going to ban imports of Chinese dogs like Pekingese, Shih Tzus, and Shar-Peis. He just rolled his eyes. I saw it clearly. And he said, "Jesus Christ," sort of under his breath. He wasn't praying, I'm sure of that. He was swearing, like The Boss had done something terrible and immoral.'"

Dash lifted both hands and said with conviction: "He's lying, Judge."

"Lying? Mr. Carouthers is lying?"

"I never said 'Jesus Christ.' I remember *exactly* what I said," Dash corrected.

"And that was..."

"I said 'Jesus *Fucking* Christ.'"

"Well, well. Thank you for clarifying, Mr. Askin. Your candor is appreciated. Now, Officer Eckholm, would you read the affidavit from Miss Clarissa Davidson?"

Dash shook his head and looked down at the table. "Wow," he muttered.

"I interviewed Miss Davidson at her office at CompuLink Machines. She told me she overheard Mr. Askin in the cafeteria refer to The Boss as, and I quote, 'a flippin' maniac.'"

"Anything to say to that, Mr. Askin?" the judge asked. "You think The Boss is a maniac?"

Outside, the chanting continued like a Greek chorus: "De-Range-Ment! De-Range-Ment!..." Dash could see some in the mob holding up small books, waving them in unison like a football team cheering section.

"There's not even a cafeteria in my building," Dash remarked. "So I don't know how much credibility ...."

"Wait one sec, Mr. Askin." The judge turned to Eckholm. "Did you check to see if there was a cafeteria, Officer Eckholm?"

"I didn't really look, Judge, but I could smell it," the Officer replied, nodding. "Sure could. Smelled like Boss Burgers."

"Alright Officer, read the last affidavit, would you?"

"I interviewed Mrs. Monica Ricardo at the elementary school. She teaches Mr. Askin's child, one Lillian Askin."

Lily gasped again, fearing she'd inflicted some horrible plague upon her father. "Mommy!" Polly shushed her.

"Mrs. Ricardo told me the child told her his dad forbids them to use The Boss's name at home."

"Terrorists are everywhere you look these days," Dash remarked, shaking his head in mock disgust.

"Hold on, now, Mr. Askin," McConicle interjected. "Let's just establish the facts. We can talk about domestic terrorism if you want. Do you or don't you forbid the use of The Boss's name in your home as this witness alleges?"

Tears were rolling down Lily's cheeks as Polly squeezed her tight. Lily was certain she'd crippled her dad's case.

"No rule, per se," Dash lied. "We don't talk much about fake celebrities or psychopaths. It's not our center of interest. We care about things like justice, honesty, integrity and so on. Remember those, Judge?"

"That's right," Polly chimed in, as if to say: "I'm still with you, Dash."

"We'll strike that remark from Mrs. Askin," McConicle declared. He turned to Eckholm. "Thank you for that evidence. I believe we've heard enough."

The judge carefully closed his ring binder and gently removed his eyeglasses before turning back to Eckholm. "Is there anything you've heard from the defendant, Officer Eckholm, that might cause you to question the veracity of these three affidavits?"

"No, sir."

"Well, thank you." McConicle slipped his glasses back on and scanned from right to left as if the hearing had an audience. "Let's now evaluate all of this evidence from a professional psychiatric standpoint. Dr. Stancil, would you take the oath?"

Stancil stood, placed his palm on the Bible, and swore to tell the truth with a simple "I do" and a couple of left-handed swats at the air near his ear that nearly knocked off his glasses.

McConicle asked: "Now, Dr. Stancil, would you state your name and occupation and any highlights of your educational achievements?"

"D-d-d-d-d-Doctor A-Avery St-St-Stancil. D-d-d-d-Doctor of sigh-sigh-sigh Psychiatry." He swatted the air a couple more times. "S-s-s-Southeast Medical you-you-University."

"We're not going to make you talk very much, Doctor. I can see you're a little nervous. I know you're not stuttering. That's banned. It's just nerves, so a 'yes' or 'no' will do. Let's get started. In your professional opinion, Dr. Stancil, does the evidence you've heard and the behavior of the defendant you've witnessed during this hearing cause you to conclude he is not living in the real world and could be a threat to himself or others?"

Stancil nodded as he swatted with both hands, shooing away something quite invisible near both of his ears. "It sir-sir-sir certainly does," he said.

"Alright. Thank you, Dr. Stancil. That's all we need. You can relax. Now, before I rule on the question of whether Dashiel Nathan Askin is Deranged or not, Mr. Askin gets two minutes to defend himself. Would you stand, sir? And no swearing or banned words, please."

As Dash pushed his chair back and stood, the three Enforcers across the table stiffened, as if Dash might lunge for McConicle's throat. In his mind, though, Dash was remembering his mother and father and how they would have loved seeing him at the hearing. How they had taught him to cherish individual rights, to do justice, to love mercy, and to walk humbly. He looked down at the carpet to gather his thoughts.

"I don't think I'll need two minutes," Dash began. "We've pretended for decades in this country that we all enjoy free speech, but we don't. Sure, it's stated in a few creepy phrases in The Ten Grudgments. Those words are so distorted and deceptive they mean nothing. Freedom of thought and expression are only for people who follow the decrees of The Boss, then inform on their neighbors to get their hands on Participation Payments. So what we actually have is freedom of propaganda, freedom of intimidation, freedom of lies. Fear and greed govern everything. I'm sure you think I'm a Boss Hater, but it's not personal. It really isn't, Judge. I'm just against the filth of corruption and disinformation, the enslavement of the mind, cults of personality, and..."

"That's enough, Mr. Askin!" the judge shouted, pounding both palms on the table so that it shook. "Sit down, sir!"

Dash sat and flashed a big smile at the judge. "Amen," said Polly in a stage whisper.

"Amen," Lily echoed softly.

McConicle calmed himself, cleared his throat, and re-established his professorial tone.

"We're gonna draw this to a close. I doubt anyone would reasonably argue that the defendant is thinking clearly. Beyond the evidence in the affidavits, his comments at this hearing are, frankly, damning. Therefore, after careful consideration and due prayer, I conclude that the defendant is Deranged, falling into the Lunatic category." Dash continued to look directly at the judge. "The comments in the affidavits that are attributed to the defendant are those of a person disconnected from reality. This is a textbook case of Deranged Lunacy. It's akin to psychosis. A sane individual would not veer into contemptuous speech that also borders on sedition, but I'm afraid Mr. Askin has done just that."

McConicle sat up in his chair and pulled his shoulders back as if he were about to issue a benediction or proclamation.

"When it comes to Deranged Lunatics," he went on, "it's my job to protect the public and protect you, Mr. Askin, from harming yourself as you think these delusional thoughts about our society and our leadership. We aim to be humanitarian in this regard. I do believe your particular form of Lunacy is temporary. I really do, despite Mr. Askin's well-known roots. So, I'm sentencing you to two years' confinement at Sanctuary Thirteen. In Jesus's name. Blessed Be The Boss. Amen."

Polly's knees buckled, and the female Enforcer swept over to help keep her erect. Tears silently flowed down Lily's face.

"Now I want you to understand, Mr. Askin, a Sanctuary is not a prison," the judge added. "Just a place to get your head straight. You'll be a DL, Category One. You can have visitors on Wednesday nights and weekends. Polly'll stay here with the little girl, for now. You'll be in the care of trained psychiatrists. As The Boss himself says, we don't hate the DLs, we pity them. I hope you'll use your time away wisely, Mr. Askin, and take Behavior Adjustment seriously so you can think clearer thoughts. Good luck to you, sir. That concludes the hearing."

Judge McConicle nodded to everyone at the table and stood, taking care to lift his black robe to avoid tripping. "That's it, I guess. Gotta pack up for my next hearing. Dr. Stancil, will you remind me to put through the Participation Payments to those folks who filed affidavits? And call Thirteen, would you, to let them know to expect a new guest? I'll get my clerk to phone CompuLink to tell them Mr. Askin won't be at work for a while."

Polly had collected herself and was smoothing her jeans. Lily had her arms around Polly's waist.

"Mrs. Askin, if you would gather some clothes and a few books for your husband if he wants. Maybe that burger book. But no razor blades and no belts, okay?"

Suddenly, Dash felt the full weight of the moment. He sat rock still, breathing slowly. The last color had drained from his face and neck. He stared out the window as if transfixed by the still-chanting mob. He knew it could have been worse, but his life was now upside down. Polly and Lily moved to embrace him from behind, saying nothing.

When Judge McConicle snapped his suitcase shut, two Enforcers reached into a bag and unfolded a white polyester straitjacket.

"It's time, Mr. Askin," one of them said.

Judge McConicle exited the house first. The two male Enforcers held up the straitjacketed Dashiel Askin by the upper arms, his gaze straight ahead. The female Enforcer carried Dash's backpack. Stancil kept swatting. A local news crew was recording everything. Thick cables ran to a white van with the words "No B.S." on its side. Up top was a small satellite dish marked "BTV Local News."

A cheer arose from the crowd, which consisted of a dozen members of the League of Christian Voters, some of whom Dash recognized as members of the local vigilante militia; others had pulled ski masks over their faces. Their lungs were still strong and their signs were held high. A few had Glocks and Berettas tucked into their belts. For the first time, Dash could read the signs. He'd seen them for decades on highway billboards and on the walls at Lily's school. "Jesus and The Boss Love America," they read.

A few waved small blue-jacketed books, which Dash recognized as The Boss's recently published volume, *The Eternal Quotations of Acton Grudge.*

The sun was bright and hot, and the air was clear. At the open door, Winston shook himself into a state of alertness as Polly and Lily stood holding each other. The chanting died out as the Enforcers folded Dash into the back seat of a black cruiser. One of the masked League members shouted: "Happy Grudgment Day, buddy!"

Everyone grinned, even Dash, who, with an exaggerated wink, offered a taunting acknowledgment to his tormentors before the car door closed and locked automatically with a sharp thud.

2

The canopy of trees swayed gently and the shafts of sunlight pulsed almost horizontally through the forest from a dimming blue sky as the Enforcer cruiser carrying Dash Askin sped along the parkway toward Sanctuary Thirteen. For most of the ride, he had withdrawn into a state of serene nothingness, to which passing vistas of the natural world were an uncorrupted balm. Gradually, though, he slipped out of his emptiness into the somethingness of his life, where actions past, present, and future merged. He felt neither pain nor regret nor fear, but he did feel alone. He thought of Mike and Katharine. Both of his parents were dissenters in their day, the formative days of Bossism. They had lived through the Big Burn and more — much more. He thought of Polly. And he thought of Lily. *Will they manage without me?*

Dash was sifting memories in the caged back seat when the Enforcer at the wheel announced that they were ten minutes away, in effect preparing him, perhaps even taunting him. *Ten minutes away from your destiny.* His meditation was over. Dash's mind placed him squarely into the cold reality of the present. A voice echoed within: "Just do what you always said you'd do."

When the officers escorted Dash up the path to the Sanctuary's main building, the sun was a bright orange ball sinking to the horizon. The place was a neatly kept campus of three-story, ivy-covered brick structures that looked like a high-class nursing home with a warehouse attached. Two eighteen-wheel trucks were parked near the warehouse. A large cursive "Welcome!" sign capped the entrance to the main building. The double entry doors bore a massive illustration of a younger version of The Boss. Dash imagined that when both doors opened from the center, slicing The Boss's septum, he would be entering the rancid sinuses and chaotic, infantile brain of Acton Grudge.

The cops guided Dash to a carpeted waiting area labeled "Admitting" as the double doors slammed shut. The air-conditioning hummed. His straitjacket pinched.

"We're gonna take off now, Dash," one of the two Enforcers said. "You're in good hands. Enjoy your stay."

"Sure," Dash responded. "Thanks for the lift."

A tall gentleman in an ill-fitting suit and tie strode briskly toward him, smiling broadly, his rubber-soled shoes squeaking on the waxed floors.

"Well, we've been expecting you. Mr. Askin, right? I'm Ron Pickett, Head of Admitting." The treacly greeting set Dash on edge. Pickett spoke with a thick Philadelphia accent. He was almost jovial. The man hadn't shaved that day, and his hair was thinning, revealing brown patches on his scalp and dandruff. "Let's get you out of that contraption," Pickett said. "Need the men's room? Can I get you a soda? A chocolate bar?"

Pickett removed Dash's straitjacket and tossed it on a chair as Dash stretched and hunched his shoulders to loosen up after the long drive.

"No. I'm okay."

"Come on into my office, then. We'll get you an ID bracelet."

Pickett motioned Dash to a chair across his desk and reached forward to snap a black metal bracelet bearing the letters DL and the numbers 6-4-8 onto Dash's right wrist. It locked.

"This has all your information and personal data, heart monitor, GPS, arrest record, social media preferences, free-speech violations, tax and income data, sleep monitor, library withdrawals, BossMart buying history, the whole nine yards," Pickett said. "Everybody loves 'em. Now, I'm just gonna take a little health history so we know if you need any medications and such. We take very good care of our residents."

From the time the hearing ended that morning, Dash had been feeling the weight of his predicament. He was entering a guarded federal institution where he could simply disappear under strange circumstances at any time, leaving Polly and Lily to fend for themselves, and the world would be clueless. Nobody would care. Bossism had created tens of millions of Passivists who go about their lives with blinders on, unwilling to witness the trajectory of the human race, maybe because it was too frightening or because they were numb and didn't care or feared they would lose their minds if they did. The Boss's goons could spread a little toxin on his cornflakes or slip trays of spoiled food to him in an unheated cell and he'd have to decide whether to give up and die of malnutrition or give up and die of hypothermia. They could double or triple his sentence, and no one would care. He was feeling alone and dazed, searching for the resolve he knew he'd need in the months to come.

"You okay, Mr. Askin?"

"Yeah, sure," Dash replied dully as he tried to re-center himself. He glanced around at the pale green walls, where two framed items caught his eye. One was a red-white-and-blue certificate that read: "Employee of the Week" and the other was a meticulously air-brushed and significantly dated color portrait of Acton Grudge.

Pickett took Dash's medical history, tapping notes on a computer keyboard. There wasn't much to say, as Dash was healthy, though one of Pickett's questions was: "Have you ever taken Halcitol?"

"No," replied Dash. "I'm extremely happy, thanks."

"Well, you may want to try it in here," Pickett whispered, leaning across the desk as if he were imparting top-secret clues to enhanced longevity. "It's a wonderful drug. It'll help you get through. Everybody swears by it." Pickett leaned back. "Can I call you Dash?"

"Yeah. It's fine."

"Good, good. So, Dash. Before we go any further, there's a great opportunity I want to discuss with you. We don't offer it to everyone at Sanctuary Thirteen. This is an exclusive. It's called an Admission, where you accept your Derangement publicly and agree to make amends in return for special treatment. As Head of Admitting, I take you into a nice, comfortable studio down the hall, just like a living room, and make a video of your personal Admission. You tell the truth about your Derangement and explain how you'll move forward like a good citizen. The video gets played on BTV so everyone knows you're now a Patriot and no longer an Enemy of the People. If you do all that, your time here inside Sanctuary Thirteen gets reduced to six months, officially. That's quite an incentive, don't you think? You can handle six months, can't you?"

Dash felt like a car buyer listening to a pushy salesman trying to get him to sign up for an extended warranty and flashy rims.

"But the thing is, Dash, you have to decide now. You get one chance. Can't do it later. It's a take-it-or-leave-it Special. Polly told me she wants you to do it. What do you think?"

"You talked to Polly?"

"Sure did. Nice lady. But she's real worried about you. Said you'd been Deranged for some time."

Dash lowered his head meditatively and kept it down, thinking how laughable it was for Pickett to put those words in Polly's mouth. She probably told him to go stuff a rancid Boss Burger.

"I'll have to think a minute," Dash said. Pickett didn't stir. After a good fifteen seconds of silence, Dash lifted his chin and started nodding.

"Yep. Okay. That sounds fine, Mr. Pickett. I think I can do a good video for you. At least I'll try. It'll go on BTV, right?"

"It sure will. That's great, Dash. Come on." Pickett was beaming as he swung around his desk. "No time like the present."

Dash had a bounce in his step as the two strode down the hall and entered a well-lit mini-studio furnished like a "Death of a Salesman" living room stage set, complete with fake windows looking out on painted clouds and a blue sky. Dash slipped behind the coffee table and took a seat on the worn brown couch while smoothing his hair. Pickett threaded a microphone to his shirt pocket.

"All you have to do, Dash, is say you made a mistake about The Boss and realize how wrong you were. You can say it any way you want, in your own words, real natural. Pretend like it's coming from your heart. But just do this at the end: say 'I made a mistake. I'm a true Patriot. I'm no longer Deranged.'"

Dash nodded. "Made a mistake. True Patriot. Not Deranged."

"You got it. You're gonna look great on TV, Dash. I can tell. Now, don't start talking til I say 'Action.'"

Pickett retreated to a stationary video camera, adjusted the zoom lens, flashed a thumbs-up to Dash, and boomed in his best Cecil B. DeMille, "And...Action!"

Dash threw a smile on his face and flipped smartly into his impression of a sparkling TV personality about to deliver really good news.

"Hi, this is Dashiel Askin. I want to tell all of you from the bottom of my heart that I misjudged The Boss. I really did. I made a mistake. I thought The Boss was a power-mad deviant who cared only about domination and submission. I admit I thought The Boss used brutality, fear, and propaganda to control a cult of personality. This was my error. I admit I was wrong. I'm here in Admitting at Sanctuary Thirteen to tell you *I now realize* my error. It's actually a lot worse than I thought, because The Boss is the anti-Christ posing as a genius con-man..."

"Cut! Cut! Cut!" Pickett bellowed. He turned swiftly to the wall behind him and mashed a red button with the side of his fist. Turning back, he growled, "Don't you move! I've called the Monitors. We're done here, Dash. You think you're so smart. Well, you're not. You're an Enemy of the People. You just proved it. And you're going to the third floor for a nice long time. Happy Grudgment Day, Dash. Blessed Be The Boss. Someday, you'll wish you hadn't done this."

Dash sat back, splayed both arms across the back of the faded couch cushions, closed his eyes, and started singing "Amazing Grace" in a mournfully slow cadence, just as he'd done dozens of times before in the shower or while putting Lily to bed.

"Y ou'll feel just a little prick." The young man who introduced himself as "your nurse" but had no name stitched onto the breast pocket of his white cotton jacket inserted a needle into Dash's right buttock.

"It'll take just a few minutes to start working. You'll feel calmer. Happier. Sleep better. More like yourself than ever. Then, we'll unstrap you."

After just ten minutes, Dash realized the kid was right. He felt like smiling for no apparent reason. He almost thanked the nurse for the Halcitol injection after they unstrapped him. Curiously, he still understood quite clearly that he was a prisoner, no matter what they called this place — Asylum, Derangement Clinic, or Brain Spa for Boss Haters. He wondered why he was happy to be a prisoner, even though, peculiarly, he still harbored raging malice for the regime and knew his detention was a lawless act. He felt happy about the paint on the walls and ceiling and happy about the pattern of the floor tiles. He was happy having a locked bracelet on his wrist. It was all very strange.

When they helped him up, a wiry, white-haired attendant handed Dash a plastic name tag that said "Dashiel" and instructed him on how and where to clip it to his shirt. As he leaned over to show where to place it, Dash felt the man's other hand slip something into the back pocket of his pants, a piece of paper perhaps. It crinkled. He turned quickly to look into the attendant's eyes and was met with the kind of exaggerated glance, including sharply raised eyebrows, that an actor might employ in a kitschy ad on BTV. Dash saw the man's name tag. It was "Caleb."

In a clear, deep Georgia accent, Caleb cautioned, "Don't never take that name tag off or they'll whup ya real good!"

"Okay," Dash promised.

This was Dash's first inkling that the Sanctuary staff might be infiltrated by dissidents of the regime. That made him especially happy. He'd heard rumors that the people rounded up and sent to the Sanctuaries, tens of thousands of them, had created an active network to weaken The Boss any way they could, through fakery or force. It was probably wishful thinking, but he asked himself: what if a secret war is being waged under everyone's noses?

Dash noticed for the first time that it was dark outside. The windows had iron bars on the inside, but it seemed that one could reach through them to twist a knob and get fresh air. The idea of fresh air made him feel happy. He thought he'd be quite happy to see what the man named Caleb had placed in his pocket, whenever he could find a private moment. He didn't dare move his hand to feel it.

A bulky, middle-aged woman whose name tag read "Angela" escorted Dash from the nurse's cubicle to a large community room. Angela wore a crucifix around her neck and had a sunny disposition. She had worked at Sanctuary Thirteen for nearly a decade, rising to the rank of Floor Captain and earning decent money in a town still struggling to regain its economic footing after the third wave of anti-migrant riots. The town's Colombian Coffee Roasting Factory was fire-bombed by the mob back then, apparently because the building featured a large billboard of the fictional South American farmer Juan Valdez and his donkey. She'd seen thousands of DLs enter the halls of Thirteen and, as far as she knew, they'd left as grateful

Patriots with a new appreciation for The Boss and "Making Things POSSible."

"All the DLs are friendly here, Mr. Askin," Angela assured him. "Let's sit for a minute so I can explain how things work at Thirteen. Everybody's getting ready for dinner. It won't take too long."

Dash took in his surroundings, and he was happy about what he saw. The community room featured oversized lounge chairs, modern table lamps, and upholstered benches arranged like a hotel lobby. The floor was a warm walnut color. Portraits of The Boss and Jesus were hanging behind a broad reception desk, along with a mini-Boss Nation flag. There were chess and checkers boards set up. Strip lights illuminated the thick wooden ceiling beams. The place was empty, and red-checked curtains framed the iron-barred windows. Dash thought he'd arrived at a two-star, Christians-only ski lodge during a drought.

"Thank you, Angela. That would be nice," Dash found himself saying with complete sincerity.

"You'll have a roommate on the men's wing of Building A. That's this building. Anti-Derangement Class is every morning at nine, in a group. And chapel prayer is every night before bed and on Sunday mornings. Behavior Adjustment is once a week. It's one-on-one and kind of intensive. The psychiatrist or a resident sees you every other day just to check in. There's a co-ed smoking and vaping room. And there's a sound-proof Purge Room where you can scream all the angry Derangement out, but you've got to reserve that ahead because there's a lot of demand. We'll issue you an electric shaver if you decide to remove that beard; no razors allowed. The rest of the time you'll be working at the Resource Recovery Center and earning bitpoints. What we do here at Thirteen is pull valuable metals out of used electric vehicles, voting machines — we no longer need those — and personal assault rifles that have passed their 'shoot-by' date. It's great therapy, Mr. Askin. Very rewarding. That's the big warehouse building you probably saw coming in. Ladies have their own wing but everyone eats together in the cafeteria in the basement of Building B. It's connected by a tunnel. There's an art room down there, where you can paint approved scenes by numbers. And there's an arcade room with games like 'Commando' and 'Afterburner.' We do have some rules, though: no Grade One vulgarity. Grade Two is okay. You know, the words you hear on BTV all the time, like the three B's. Those are fine."

"Bullshit," "bastard," and "bitch," Dash said knowingly.

"Yes, sir."

Angela leaned in and confided: "The men here are very respectful. They know I don't really like the B words. Profanity is so common these days. I wish The Boss would cool that. I just barely tolerate the three B's, except when one particular B word is directed at me. If they call me a b-i-t-c-h, I turn right around and pop 'em one real hard. Just a little warning." For emphasis, she pounded her right fist into the palm of her left hand, causing the flesh of her upper arms to jiggle. Then she directed a big-eyed smile at Dash.

"Oh, I almost forgot," Angela said. "There's a library with a nice rotating collection of approved books."

"I love approved books," Dash said cheerily. "Hey, that's another B word!"

"Why, yes it is. But we *like* the word 'book.' It's just that we don't like what's *inside* every book. We've got the good ones here in the library. Like Old Westerns, Biographies of Approved Role Models, and Murder Mysteries. Also, Bibles and the Dummies series on Heating, Ventilation, and Air Conditioning. Some old Popular Mechanics magazines, too. One time they brought in thirty National Geographics. There was a stampede! Lord, I'll never forget that."

"Oh, that's nice," said Dash. "What about phone calls and visits?"

"One weeknight and one weekend day for visitors. Two phone calls a week, ten minutes max. The phone booth is on the hall. If you hear it ringing, pick up. Just remember we record the calls."

"For quality assurance, I'm guessing."

"Why that's right!" Angela exulted. "You'll fit in just fine here, Mr. Askin."

"So Angela, let me ask: what are bitpoints?"

"Oh, that's our Sanctuary money, our cash. With bitpoints, you can buy sundries and snacks at the canteen and do your laundry and stuff. But the value of a bitpoint rises and falls just like the bitdollar. So you need to watch that."

"You mean if the bitdollar crashes or I don't have any bitpoints, I can't wash my clothes?"

"Oh, it'll never crash, like a full crash. No. Everyone has confidence in the bitdollar, and you should, too. But you have to earn your bitpoints, I mean unless you want to smell bad. One capful of LaundryPro With Extra Phosphates costs only two bitpoints, and you can't go around smelling bad. It's forbidden. They can send you out to Fumigation, and you don't want that."

"No, ma'am. And where's Fumigation?"

"At all the old migrant camps."

Angela escorted Dash down the elevator, along a basement hall, and into the windowless cafeteria, where she showed him how to order from the touchscreens. Staring at him were dozens of color photos, and he soon learned why every one of them looked nauseating. The cafeteria vendor was Burger Czar, a chain he'd avoided his entire life and forbidden Lily to frequent because the best-selling and most-advertised item was the Boss Burger. It was a towering stack of ground Angus beef, Alabama jack cheese, Pacifica iceberg lettuce, pickles, Nevada jalapeño peppers, and bourbon-flavored Boss Sauce. You could also order jumbo cod nuggets, Texas fries, Carolina slaw, and barbecued chicken Drum-Drums — ground chicken meat pressed into the shape of turkey drumsticks. And blondies for dessert.

Dash's stomach turned, but he made a few selections, picked up his Drum-Drums and fries at the counter according to his number, and sat alone. He was hungry and ate fast. Discreetly, he reached into his back pocket and fished out a folded piece of paper with three printed words that he glanced at under the table near his lap: "Don't Trust Nobody."

It was odd, not quite what he'd expected, and Dash began to doubt the glimmer of hope he'd felt when the paper was inserted into his pocket. Had Caleb meant that Thirteen was crawling with undercover informants posing as patients? And what about the double-negative? Did Caleb really mean "trust everyone?"

Dash looked at the blondie on his tray and suddenly felt ill. He began to sweat. He pushed out his chair, hustled to the men's room, and threw up. He felt much better after cleaning himself, washing his face, and checking the mirror. He wasn't sure if it was a reaction to the Halcitol, the Drum-Drums or the anxiety that he might die inside Sanctuary Thirteen of clogged arteries, salmonella or state-administered poison. Still, nothing seemed amiss as soon as the worry passed. He felt happy.

That first night, Dash went to bed early and dreamed he was a bitpoint billionaire lounging on the shore of a turquoise sea while Polly and Lily built a sand castle resembling an oozing Boss Burger. When he opened his eyes in the morning, he saw the lime-green walls, the framed portrait of The Boss, and the barred window in his room. You are nothing more than a DL in a chain of drab prisons masquerading as mental institutions, he thought. All the DLs at Thirteen are either Boss Haters like me or undercover agents reporting to a paranoid regime on the silent opposition. He recalled that for the felony of thinking for himself, he'd been separated from his family and sent off in a straitjacket by a Boss-owned judge. Even so, Dash still felt happy; the Halcitol seemed that strong. How odd, he thought.

Dash turned in his bed and for the first time saw he was not alone. Across the room, an older man sat on the edge of the other twin bed in a pair of gray pajamas stamped with red letters that said: "Sanctuary 13 Football." He'd been watching Dash, and he smiled a languid smile.

"Get your Halcitol shot?" the man asked.

"Yesterday."

"Later, when they're not lip-reading through the two-way mirrors, I'll tell you a secret about that stuff. Not here inside Stalag Thirteen, though. Bet they treated you real nice yesterday, like family, right?"

"Sort of. Why do you say that?"

"'Cause that's what they want you to think. Home away from home. Take the flowers in the vase on the end table. Fake as fuck. DL is just another term for political prisoner, and they're gonna try to break you in very subtle ways. Just a small warning I issue to all the newcomers. They try to break everybody. All the Behavior Adjustment shit and the group classes. You'll see. So, what'd you do to land in the Gulag?"

Dash didn't want to divulge too much. He remembered the note in his pocket.

"The usual, I guess," he said.

"Crossed The Boss, I reckon. If you get out of line, you're suddenly nuts and need medicine. By the way, I'm LeBeau. Clary LeBeau. Clary's a family name. Most people call me LeBeau. Somewhere way back, I was Canadian, I guess. Maybe French. Shoulda stayed." He extended his hand and Dash shook it.

LeBeau was thin but strong-looking. He wore a short beard that framed his sunken cheeks. What was that look? Wisdom? Experience? Desperation? Dash thought he saw all three in LeBeau's face.

"I'm Dash, short for Dashiel. Dashiel Askin."

"Dash. I like that. Like you're ready to sprint. We'd all like to dash outta this..." LeBeau cut himself off, put his feet back up and reclined on his bed with both hands cupped behind his head. "It's not so bad here. Anyway, what did ya say about The Boss that pissed everybody off?"

Dash didn't answer.

"It's fine. You don't know who you can trust, who's gone undercover in here trying to sniff out seditionists and socialists. Or who's a weak, sniveling little DL tryin' to scratch up some extra bitpoints by snitching to the staff. We've got a few of those."

Dash was silent.

"Don't worry," LeBeau said, "I don't take it personal. In time, you'll figure out who you can trust."

"I'll figure it out."

"It's kinda clever of them, when you think about it. You don't know if I'm a snitch and I don't know if you're a snitch. When you figure it out, let me know. Just be aware that anything you say in here that sounds vaguely disloyal to you-know-who is probably gonna find its way to the Superintendent. Best leave those conversations for Exercise Hour outside. But I can help you, Dash. That's what we do in here. We help each other. Once you learn you can trust me, I can help. That's all I'm sayin." LeBeau had his head turned and was looking straight at Dash when he said this, trying to judge the reaction, but there was none.

Dash imagined the Sanctuaries were full of people who shared his defiant streak, men and women courageous or foolhardy enough to put principle before personal safety, people who tried to set an example for their kids. On the surface, at least, LeBeau seemed like one of them. While the Enforcers drove Dash upstate, he'd been thinking he'd find kindred spirits at Thirteen, rule breakers. He missed Polly and Lily, but he knew they would want him to be as resolute tomorrow and the next day as he had been during the Derangement Hearing. He wanted to believe they were looking up to him and expecting him to act with purity of spirit and unflagging courage, no matter what. He held onto that thought. Maybe it was the Halcitol keeping him from being engulfed by a wave of despair and self-pity.

The only way forward, Dash reasoned, was to accept one's fate with equanimity and to be exactly the person you'd want to look up to, right to the end. That meant seizing the opportunity of being a DL, finding the other Boss Haters, encountering activists willing to work against the regime, and sowing confusion, dissension, and doubt about The Boss and his squalid movement. And, finally, believing that The Boss's propaganda machine will one day run out of gas or corrode from within. It had to.

Why worry about LeBeau? Was an undercover agent inside Thirteen going to reveal something about Dashiel Askin that he hadn't already revealed at his Derangement Hearing? Shit, he thought, I'm a political prisoner already, just like LeBeau said. Why tiptoe around worrying that the goon squad will punish me for thoughts more seditious than the ones that landed me here in the first place? Besides, he thought, LeBeau makes me happy — or, again, it's just the Halcitol.

The one thing Dash would never divulge to LeBeau or anyone else was his work as a self-appointed saboteur inside CompuLink. Only Polly knew what he'd been up to, and they spoke of it rarely and only in code. CompuLink's patented software sat inside every machine learning program in the world outside of China. Gradually, Dash came to the realization that the programs and algorithms the company was selling were normalizing authoritarianism, creating a built-in tendency to reply to queries as if it was all perfectly normal to curtail free speech, imprison dissidents, flood social media with disinformation, and shove aside or bury any references to liberal democracy.

The autonomic intelligence machines were like six-year-olds who believed everything they heard on the playground because there was no adult around to correct their false assumptions and mistaken impressions. It consumed Dash, so he took it upon himself to clandestinely eliminate those tendencies inside CompuLink's code without leaving fingerprints. The company suspected nothing, but Dash understood that his window of opportunity was limited. One day, they would figure it out. Or the regime would. When Polly occasionally asked him if he'd done any "tinkering" that day at work — their code word for sabotage — she might as well have been asking nonchalantly if her husband had busted into a weapons factory, planted explosives, and escaped alive to keep democracy from being erased from history.

LeBeau interrupted Dash's moment of calculation: "Did you meet Caleb Jones?"

"The guy who gave me my name tag?"

"Yeah. Did he give you anything else?"

Dash smiled. "It didn't make sense. It had a double-negative."

LeBeau burst into prolonged laughter, and tears flooded his eyes.

"What's that supposed to mean?" Dash inquired. "Who the hell is Caleb Jones?"

LeBeau calmed himself. "Let's just say Caleb is a good guy. And it means you can trust me. That's all I'll say for now."

Dash looked into LeBeau's washed-out eyes. He saw no point in prolonging the cautious testing phase of his presence at Sanctuary Thirteen and said in a stage whisper: "Well, then, I trust you."

"That's good, cuz you got no choice. Like I said, we need each other. And when you need someone, you gotta take a risk and trust 'em or you might as well curl up into a ball and give up."

"I have to ask, are we being recorded in here?"

"Not always. Take these bracelets. We're pretty sure they're not recording and transmitting our words. Enough shit that people say ends up on the Superintendent's desk, though, so there must be devices here and there in the rooms. They're well hidden. But the two-way mirrors. Watch out for them. We know they read lips."

"You asked earlier what I'd said about The Boss," Dash offered.

"I just wondered how you describe your own insanity. We're Deranged Lunatics, remember? If you asked me what got me in here, I'd say, 'I don't eat bullshit for breakfast, lunch, and dinner. I know the difference between blissful ignorance and willful ignorance. I use my fuckin' brain. And I don't take orders from any self-appointed bully boy selling fear and grievance.'"

"What if they just heard you say that?"

LeBeau had himself another big laugh. "I've told it to 'em a hundred times. Right to their ugly faces. Not sayin' anything I haven't said before. It's liberating, even in prison. Yeah, they've doubled my sentence a couple times. I don't give a shit. I refuse to live in fear. It'll age you. Not good for your body. Not good for your soul."

"How long have you been at Thirteen, LeBeau?"

"Six years this January. Did they try to get you to record an Admission when you got here?"

"They did." Now, Dash was the one laughing. "Gosh, did I have fun. You should have seen Pickett. I made him think I was all primed to be repentant and do a first-class Admission. I said I'd misjudged The Boss with the camera running and then I said I realized he was worse than I thought, a con man and the anti-Christ."

"You hit a nerve there, brother. Jesus is The Boss's co-pilot. We're a Christian society now, right?"

"I guess so. Either a Christocracy or a kleptocracy."

"Any one of those, but I'd go with Christocracy. The Bible Belt got so wide The Boss, God bless him, had no choice but to wear it around his fat middle like a heavyweight champ."

Dash opened up. "You want to know why I'm here? I'll tell you. And they can listen all they want. I'm here because my parents showed me how to fight back, right from the first

Big Burn. I've thought about the Sanctuaries for years. I knew I'd be here one day. I didn't want to risk it until my daughter was old enough to understand. She's a good kid. She's twelve now, and I'm pretty sure she'll make it. Sometimes, I think I was meant to be here — my destiny, you know?"

"Wait, wait. Askin. You mean the trials? Is that them?"

Dash nodded.

"Shit. Sorry, man."

"Never mind. There's something I need to ask you."

"Sure."

Dash rose, sat beside LeBeau, cupped his hand over his mouth, and whispered, "I've heard there might be an Underground in here. True?"

LeBeau lifted his index finger to his lips. "Gotta practice a little of our own Shut-up-ism on that one."

Dash nodded and started to get up, but LeBeau grabbed his arm.

"We'll talk outside. They'll give you a tour of the Resource Recovery Center this morning so they can tell you all about our Recycling for Christ program. Find me at Exercise Hour outside. It's just before lunch. I'll look for you. But right now, we gotta make it to breakfast. If you're late, you go hungry. And you better at least mouth the words to Grace before you eat or they'll swoop in and ask" — LeBeau put on a syrupy Angela-like voice — "'Now, son, you feelin' unhappy today?'"

Dash noticed that his happiness meter was still flashing green. The idea of touring the Resource Recovery Center pleased him. He couldn't wait to dive into the work. He'd felt just as relaxed talking to LeBeau as he had speaking to Angela. He concluded that Halcitol wasn't a personality-erasing drug. It seemed to enhance his desire to act, to feed his somethingness. I'm still who I am, he reassured himself. I still despise The Boss, and I still want revenge. It calmed his mind to know he hadn't been altered somehow. Dash was more than happy. He felt emboldened. His desire to do something important with his time at Sanctuary Thirteen was at a glorious peak. If he only knew what.

3

The Resource Recovery Center at Sanctuary Thirteen was a pointillist canvas with hundreds of animated DLs working the lines in orange coveralls and royal blue neoprene gloves, some using hand tools and others operating robotic jaws. It assaulted Dash's senses. Even with his mandatory noise-dampening safety ear muffs, the place was as loud as a monster-truck demolition derby.

The plant housed three assembly lines, with the DLs working as professional scavengers. When China banned the export of rare earth metals, the ones needed to make computer chips and high-tech assemblies, The Boss mounted a campaign to extract everything usable from discarded electronic devices, crashed drones, electric cars, out-of-use voting machines, computers, and outdated small weapons of all sorts. Before any of it went into the crusher, everything worth saving had to be stripped out by hand. The Boss or his aides came up with the idea of using Deranged Lunatics as a scavenger labor force. It was a two-fer. In addition to neutralizing and isolating the regime's critics, the Sanctuaries performed essential work to support the Bosseconomy.

Dash saw workers cut sections out and drop them into a set of bins behind each workstation. They were marked Platinum, Palladium, Rhodium, Microchips, Condensers, Copper, Aluminum, GPS Systems, and Audio Parts. Tractor-trailer trucks unloaded intact equipment at the salvage plant's bays and departed with barrels of sorted parts and leftover scrap metal pressed into cubes.

He was happy to see all of it, but as his guide showed him around, Dash wondered how so many supposedly crazy people could be so efficient. When he learned that none of the scavenger DLs were compensated, except in occasional bitpoint bonuses, he put the question to LeBeau during Exercise Hour: how could the DLs allow themselves to be so exploited?

LeBeau shrugged. "Why would they pay us? What the hell would we do with the money, Dash? We're Lunatics, remember? Nothing we do or say has value. Can't have a bank account. Can't buy stuff at the canteen unless you've earned bitpoints. They don't take cash. And we've got no way to support anyone on the outside who needs our help. Free labor? Yeah. Part of The Boss's game. It's another reason we fight back when we can."

"I need to talk to you about that," Dash said.

"We will. Let's walk."

The two ambled along a park-like path lined with outdoor exercise equipment, well away from the uniformed Monitors, who chain-vaped and carried billy clubs and yellow zip ties latched to their wide black belts. The stone walls at the perimeter were topped by coils of razor wire.

LeBeau asked about Dash's work on the outside.

"Computer and software engineering. Programming research. Autonomic Intelligence."

"Well, you're one elite son-of-a-bitch, aren't you," LeBeau mocked, half in jest.

Dash frowned, and LeBeau let it go.

"You didn't have a Boss Nation flag at your house to keep up appearances?"

"No."

"Good for you, but you must have had that little plastic card with The Ten Grudgments in your pocket, right?"

"I don't do many of the Required Discretionaries. I didn't carry one. But listen, LeBeau, why all these questions? You sound like the judge who sent me up here."

"Ah, never mind." LeBeau waved both hands like he was erasing the air. "I trust you, man. In fact, we could use someone who knows his way around computers."

"And by 'we' you mean...."

"I mean hell, yes, there's an Underground. It probably exists at all the Sanctuaries, but I can't be sure anymore. We lost communication. We had a secret mobile phone for a long time, maybe a year, smuggled in by someone on the Sanctuary staff. Guess who? Caleb Jones. Anyway, we used the phone to connect to the Lit Web, not to make calls. It's where a lot of encrypted traffic happens among Boss Haters, but you gotta be careful as hell. For security, we erased the phone every night. When it was on, we got connected to the outside world through a clever link to Thirteen's main router. It's right in Building A. One of the early DLs set it up so we could get to the Web through the phone's browser but not to a cell tower. But we're fucked now, 'cause the staff found the phone and confiscated it."

"I do a lot of work on novel communications," Dash mused. "Maybe I could get us up and running again."

"That'd be a massive fuckin' help. I mean it. But how the hell you gonna do it?"

"I'll give it some thought. I've been known to come up with creative little hacks."

"We may be weak in here, but we're not impotent," LeBeau said. "There are some smart DLs at Thirteen. And I know we're not alone. There are lots of other Sanctuaries. Did you ever hear about the drag queen incident?"

Dash was mystified.

"Oh, shit. Last Thanksgiving, some of our DLs with BTV privileges were watching the parade in New York. All of a sudden, a massive balloon of a drag queen floats across the screen. I wasn't there, but they told me everyone watching BTV stood and cheered. God, I wish I'd seen it. We had no idea who pulled off that genius prank. So much for The Boss's Sunday School sobriety. They told me the camera lingered on the drag queen balloon for maybe twenty seconds before the censor mashed the kill button. I can hear him now, sittin' in his booth and suddenly jumpin' outta his seat shouting, 'It's a drag queen!'"

"Is that it?" Dash asked, perplexed. "That's what you do? Pranks? It doesn't exactly crush The Boss. What's the point, LeBeau?"

"Shit, no, that's not all we do. But it was a huge injection of morale. It can get goddamn depressing in here, dealing with The Boss's crap. It takes a lot of self-motivation just to avoid giving up. I'm guessin' a third of the DLs at Thirteen are active in the Underground. Some put more into it than others. It depends on how risky they think the work is. Everything we try is called an FTB. It means Fuck The Boss. We coordinate with other Sanctuaries when we can, but like I said, right now we've got no communication. I think we keep at it because we've got Halcitol in our veins, but don't tell them that."

"What about the other two-thirds of the DLs? Do they know what's going on?"

"They know but they keep their mouths shut. Like everyone else, they're just too frightened. Or they quietly suggest FTBs for someone else to do because they don't wanna get too involved. They wanna get outta Thirteen early, on good behavior. I can't exactly blame 'em."

"Tell me about the DLs who're active. Which ones? Can I meet them?"

"Yeah. In time. We have a brain trust, the BT. You'd think there'd be lots of people from the regime in here who fell out of favor or hit a wall and gave up. And there are some. But most are just Nobody's. That's what they call themselves: the Nobody's. These are good folks who just decided the BS from the regime was too fuckin' deep. And they took a stand. Regular folks. Nobody important. Nobody you'd know. I'm talking about a park ranger whose work was shifted from saving wildlife to guarding pipelines. He said 'fuck that.' You know, meteorologists who refused to pretend all the tornadoes were normal. Fuck that. There's an immigration lawyer whose clients were citizens and got deported anyway after the riots. Some teachers and librarians. I love those people. They just want kids to be curious and not little fuckin' robots. Or they said hell no on all the book burning. Those are people with spine, right? We also have some scientists, a doctor, an ex-spy, a military guy. They let me stay in the BT because I know the ropes around here."

"It gives me a little hope."

"Damn right it does. One of the biggest groups is journalists. You know, The Boss sued all the best ones after they weakened the libel laws. It was a bloodbath. All the ones not inside a Sanctuary work for BTV and kiss The Boss's ass."

"So tell me, LeBeau, what kinds of FTBs would you *want* to do if you could?"

"We've got five categories, or had five until we lost the phone: Sabotage, Espionage, Escape, Fucking and Royal

Fucking. The first three…well, you need a shit-load of guts and smarts and plain luck to pull them off. We gave up on Escape. We tried, but it never worked. It was a waste of our energy. But the last two? The Fuckings? Those are the fun ones. All the DLs love 'em, but they take a lot of creativity, plus luck."

"A Fucking? Like mocking The Boss?"

"Yeah, but not only The Boss. Any of his thought-control bullshit. These aren't just games we play, Dash. It's more than a drag queen balloon. We wanna chisel away at the connection between The Boss and his followers. Unmask him, you know? Prod him into an impulsive overreaction."

"Break the bond of trust."

"Exactly, the bond of trust."

Dash wanted to know more about the Brain Trust, and he coaxed names out of LeBeau.

"We don't do any Fuckings unless the Brain Trust agrees, or most of 'em. They all have some kind of expertise. I know how to take apart and put together a car engine blindfolded, for whatever that's worth. There's a guy named Jim Connolly. He was a lieutenant colonel who served with something called the Joint Military Staff, and he fought the Chinese in the Beaufort Sea. There's Andy Fineman, an environmental chemist. He's the one who rang the alarm about toxic rain from cloud seeding. Let's see. Sue Romano is an architect and designer. Ricky Tester's an engineer like you. There's Max Willen. He's something I'd never heard of, a public health psychiatrist. Go figure. Roz Pear was a correspondent for the Post who covered the Baltics War. She's got balls, that lady. Eleanor Ruby's was a Hollywood screenwriter. Clever as fuck. She was blackballed when BTV took over. Let me think. Yeah. Rashad Ellison was a spook, an intelligence officer. I think he said he was stationed in Turkey or somewhere like that. He has some stories, man. Gilbert Hersh, a heart surgeon who used to build aerobatic airplanes on the side. He wanted to steal components from the Resource Recovery Center to build a drone. It was a great idea, but we couldn't find a place to hide it."

Dash wondered how much the Sanctuary staff knew about the Underground.

"They suspect something, but they're pretty clueless. We've got one ace, though, and it's Caleb. Now there's a guy with a story. He used to be a farmer on the coastal plain and lost everything when the flooding started. He watched his entire life's work get covered in a foot of mud and silt, and he had no insurance at all because it just got too expensive. He was pretty pissed off that nobody did a fuckin' thing to prevent it. Not only did nothing but actively encouraged it. Talk to him about that sometime. You'll get an earful. Had to move his family to higher ground. He thought the mountains would be safer, so he came up here. But he needed work, so he got the Super at Thirteen to hire him. Caleb's a genius actor, and he convinced the Super he was a full-on Boss ass-kisser and too stupid to be a threat. Secretly, you know, his goal was to help the Boss Haters. Payback, right? He's being watched like a hawk, though. They do random checks on all the staff. Caleb needs to be real careful."

"The note he slipped me. It said 'Don't Trust Nobody.' What was that supposed to mean?"

"He does that to everybody. If you're a fake DL sent in under cover by the Super to collect intelligence on us, we figure you'll ignore the note and just chat up everyone to vacuum information about what's going on with the DLs. But if you're *not* an informant, Caleb figures you'll be wary, quiet, slow to connect. And he's right. That was you, Dash. You held it close to the vest. So I figured we could trust you. It's not easy doing what we do in here. We're on a knife's edge. The Super suspects something, but, like I said, most of the staff are not the brightest lights. They can be brutal when you act up. I've been straitjacketed and put in the Hooch more times than I can count."

"The Hooch?"

"The Seclusion Room. Solitary. A windowless padded room. Everything's black, padded, and soundproof. Sensory deprivation and all that."

"Sorry."

"Yeah, the Hooch is a treat. Five stars. You gotta book well in advance. They want you to go nuts in there, lose your mind for real, so they can tranquilize you. But I get real zen. It's not too hard. When a DL starts to push back — saying 'Fuck The Ten Grudgments' and such — the Super can come down hard."

"Tell me about Halcitol," Dash said. "What are they trying to do with it?'

"Yeah, Halcitol. Here's that little secret I mentioned. It makes you happy and all. But it also acts like a stimulant. It helps you focus. It's like an attention-deficit med. Makes the work at Resource Recovery tolerable. But it also gives you enough energy to work at night if you're doing something for the Underground. They don't give the shots regularly. It's too expensive. So they ask you: 'How you feeling today? Are you happy?' If you tell 'em you're kinda down or pissed off, they give you another Halcitol."

Dash and LeBeau paused at a set of sit-up benches and pretended to work out.

"Why do they want us to feel happy?" Dash inquired.

"Think about it. The regime can't tolerate uprisings or escapes from Sanctuaries. So they make sure we're happy enough to want to stay put and go to Behavior Adjustment whistling jingles. If we all got pissed off and tried to break out, that would scare the shit out the Passivists outside these walls — the regulars at The Church of The Boss. They really do think we're a bunch of psychos."

"Two realities."

"Yeah, two realities."

"What about you, LeBeau? What did you do on the outside besides take apart car engines?"

"Ran an auto body shop. I was working class all the way. But you know, I'm just an ornery sumbitch who doesn't like to be lied to. I don't like con men. I don't like folks tellin' me what to do and what to think — especially what to think. I'm 'live and let live' all the way, you know? And this manliness shit? Fuck it. Treat all God's creatures equal. Compassion. I don't get off on dominating people. I'm about forgiveness, mercy and the like. That's not pussy stuff to me. The old Jesus, remember Him?"

"Yeah, I do. That was before they made him into a cartoon character. A long time ago..."

After Dash put down a Super Boss Burger and fries for lunch, Angela pulled him aside and asked the question LeBeau had warned him about: "How are you feeling today, Mr. Askin? Are you happy?"

It was just Day Two since his Halcitol shot, and Dash worried about getting too much of the drug into his body.

"Happy as a clam in high water," he answered.

"Well, if you feel low at any point, just let me know, Mr. Askin."

"I will, Angela. I promise. Can you check me tomorrow?"

"Of course. And it's good that you're fine now, because we have a treat." Angela looked like she was going to hand Dash a winning lottery ticket. "Your first Behavior Adjustment meeting is in ten minutes!"

Dash suddenly felt like his little dinghy had sprung a leak. "Ah, sure. Behavior Adjustment."

"I'll introduce you to Dr. Armstrong. You'll like him."

They walked down three flights of stairs and into a wide tunnel that connected the main building to a wing of offices. Dash noticed that every door had either a dark-tinted window or one secured with safety glass and steel mesh. A few people were on the hall shuttling files back and forth. Dash kept smiling but his guard was up.

At Room 207, Angela stopped. The sign read: "Behavioral Health." She knocked, and Dash found himself facing a crew-cut bruiser, roughly his age, wearing a white short-sleeved shirt and a modest beer belly. The introductions were warm, and everyone smiled.

"Dr. Armstrong will take good care of you," Angela beamed as she departed.

Armstrong's colorless office had an over-the-hill brown leather couch, two side chairs, a desk, and a computer. From the couch, Dash looked at the single piece of framed art on the wall. It was Richard Armstrong's gold-edged medical degree from the American College of Osteopathic Medicine. Directly across from him, behind Armstrong's desk chair, was a sheet of framed glass with the dim glaze characteristic of two-way mirrors. He knew one when he saw one.

If they're watching, Dash thought, I'd better give these bastards a good show. Armstrong tried to soothe Dash with a warm-butter-biscuit introduction.

"Our goal, Mr. Askin, is to get you out of here and back to your wife and kids as soon as possible. We meet every week to see how you're progressing on our Behavior Adjustment Scale. 'Course, you start at the lowest, H&D, 'Hostile and Defiant.' But that's just Day One. We assume you've come to Sanctuary Thirteen somewhat unhappy. It's normal. Did you have your Halcitol shot? That should help. You can have more whenever you want it. Anyway, with our weekly sessions, you can earn your way all the way up to C&S, 'Compliant and Submissive.' That's our goal. You get bitpoints, too, so you can shop at the canteen. Sometimes, we run Bitpoint Specials, so watch for those."

"I'll be very cooperative," Dash lied. "I love Specials. Besides, nobody wants to get me out of here more than me."

"That's a great attitude. Can I call you Dash?"

Dash nodded.

"Good. Let's get started with something that should be easy for you. We always start with it: The Ten Grudgments."

Dash knew The Ten Grudgments by heart. He'd memorized them two decades before when The Boss decided that the long-running BTV series "What's Wrong With *Them?*" hadn't sufficiently solidified his grip on the minds of his subjects. He ordered everyone to memorize and live by The Ten Grudgments and to carry plastic cards so they could refer to them when in doubt about how to manage life.

"Can you recite the First Grudgment, Dash?"

Dash glanced at the two-way mirror, behind which, he was certain, sat brainwashers-in-training or maybe the Super himself. He experienced a surge of determination, reminding himself to "just do what you always said you'd do."

"Sure can," Dash said. He recited from memory:

Modernity Breeds Depravity.

"Yes, exactly. And what would you say modernity is?"

"Whatever isn't traditional, like the freedom to think in new ways."

"Uh-huh. Does modernity hate the past and hate the way we've always done things?"

"Hate it? I think it's just about modern forms of expression, new ways of living, experimentation."

"And is that good or bad?"

Dash knew the response that would promote him from "Hostile" to "Submissive," but he wasn't about to say it.

"I've got nothing against tradition, Doc, but some people want us to think the nonconformity that comes with modernity is at war with tradition. The two can live side by side, in my opinion."

"And who wants us to think they're at war?"

"Really, Doc? Let's see. Acton Grudge, for one."

"I see." Armstrong picked up his clipboard and scratched out a brief note. His voice was still soothing, nurturing, like a middle school teacher looking for a raise from the Principal. "What makes you think new, modern thinking and tradition can live side by side? You don't see that modern life wants to *replace* traditional ways, to *bury* tradition for all time? Ever think of that?"

"That's your assumption. Not mine."

"I see." Armstrong scratched another note. "Let's move on to the Second Grudgment. Do you recall it, Dash?"

"Of course." He recited:

Action Before Thought.

"And can you explain that to me?"

"Not really," Dash said, staring at Armstrong.

"Nothing comes to mind?"

"Okay, I'll take a wild guess. I'm not *ever* supposed to think for myself. I'm supposed to adhere to Shut-up-ism and do what I'm told."

"Correct. Obedience requires action, not thought. It doesn't require sitting around dreaming up options. This is a society of doers, right? That's what made America great. We see a forest in our way, we chop it down and build roads! We drive a drill into the earth and up comes oil and gas. We see someone suspicious at our front door, we take 'em out. If you stop to ask questions, you've lost before even starting. You're not a man if you sit around ruminating all day, are you Dash? You're not a man if you have to sit and think before you act. Real men *act*."

"So I hear. It's also the best way to be rash, impulsive, exercise poor judgment, and accidentally kill people, wouldn't you say, Doc?"

"Hmmm. Do you see The Boss as impulsive?"

"No, I don't. True impulsiveness takes intelligence."

Armstrong's tone flipped. He scowled. "Alright, Dash. Not a great start." He picked up his clipboard again. "We've got some work to do on that one. But let's move on. How about the Third Grudgment?"

Dash sat still for a moment, his chin to his chest and eyes closed, as if searching his memory. He knew Number Three perfectly. Number Three was the essence of Grudge-Speak: grandiose, threatening, and bizarrely contradictory. Anyone who quoted Number Three with pride hadn't a clue what it meant, and anyone who derided it in public as nonsensical risked arrest and punishment. The thing was, if you privately pissed all over The Boss, you also risked being slapped with a DL order and sent to a Sanctuary because someone who overheard you would rat you out. And if you were well known or a celebrity and publicly pissed on The

Boss, or if you were, say, a recalcitrant army officer, the Chief Law and Order Officer would dispatch Enforcers to arrest you. Then they'd stage a show trial on BTV with four acts and an intermission. It was all about setting good examples. Dash turned to Armstrong and forced an obsequious smile.

"Number Three," Dash said, reciting:

Free Speech Is Without Limit; Malicious Dissent Is Not

"Very nice. Do you have questions about Number Three, Dash? Does it make sense to you?"

"Perfectly," Dash replied, glancing again at the two-way mirror. "It's perfect Doublespeak. It runs in diametrically opposite directions at the same time. It defies the laws of physics, reason, and wisdom. It obeys only the laws of stupidity and mendacity. And it's the basis of Shut-up-ism, which was created to control free speech, not free it."

"Well, well, well, Dash. That was quite a speech. You certainly seem Deranged right now. Do you feel angry? Do you feel bitter? Would you like to scream it out?"

"How could I feel angry, Doc? I'm on Halcitol. Everything's cool."

Armstrong was at his clipboard again, scratching away. "So, we will return to Number Three at some point. Maybe take our next session on Three alone. It's an important one. For now, though, we'd better move on to the Fourth Grudgment."

"Yep. An easy one." Dash recited:

America for Americans

"Nothing ambiguous there, right Dash?"

"Not ambiguous at all. It means no migrants, no vermin, no atheists, no tainted blood, no non-Whites unless you're a citizen whose parents were citizens."

All this was true, sufficient, and well-recited, but Dash had developed a nagging itch from the time he entered Armstrong's office that prevented him from leaving well enough alone. The itch was vibrating, singing opera in his head, flashing colored lights. It wanted urgent attention. Thus, he pressed on without a moment of caution, smiling directly at the two-way mirror as if it was a TV camera and he was performing at an audition. Dash was like a four-year-old singing a burger ad jingle from memory.

"No handicapped people, no Jews, no Muslims, no nose rings, no fags, no poets, no purple hair, no uppity women, no free thinkers, no Chinese, no weaklings, no intermarriage,…"

Armstrong grabbed his clipboard and pointed it at Dash. His hand was shaking. "Now just hold on, Mr. Askin! You are way out of line. On Numbers One to Four, I'm putting you down as 'Hostile and Defiant.' You and I will be working on these for *quite* a while. I can assure you of that." He wrote a long note on the clipboard.

"I don't know what came over me, Doc."

Armstrong shifted into interrogation mode. His easy demeanor was gone.

"Judging from your last answer, you seem to think Jews are discriminated against, don't you. You're badly misinformed, Mr. Askin. What makes you think there's discrimination?"

"I'm not talking about legal discrimination, Doc. I'm talking about hatred and hostility. And it goes way beyond Jews. Maybe you don't see it, but it sure as hell happens, and we all know why. You want an example? Just take the League of Christian Voters."

"The League welcomes all faiths. Surely know this."

The itch remained. "Yeah, everyone with blind faith in a perverted Christianity. Take the Tenth Grudgment, for example. Shall I go there?"

"Just hold on. We'll get there. I have to fill out a form. I need to know how deep your Derangement is across all the Grudgments and what else turns you inside out. I have to submit an Individualized Re-education Plan to deal with you and get you back on track, because right now you're a lost soul. We've got a lot of work ahead of us. Okay, Number Five."

"Yeah, five." Dash recited:

Beware the Plotters.

"Do you know who the Plotters are, Mr. Askin?"

"Yes, I do. Plotters are everywhere you look. Probably under your desk right now. Maybe they're lurking in the men's room. Bossism is all about paranoia, Doc. We're all besieged, under constant threat, and so we've all got a responsibility to sniff out people we think threaten us, and run straight to an Enforcer, and turn them in. Or call the Participation Hotline and get a fat reward. Did I nail it, Doc?"

"Are you being sarcastic, sir?"

"No sarcasm intended, Doctor Armstrong," Dash lied.

"Do you think there are no Enemies of the People in this country? No one conspiring to undo everything we've built? That would be naive. If I had to guess, I'd say you yourself, at this moment, are an Enemy of the People. And that makes me suspect you might be a Plotter."

"That would be complete Lunacy..."

"And that's why you're here, Dash. This process right here? We used to call it 'De-Derangement,' but we had to stop using that label because it sounded too much like stuttering, and The Boss banned stuttering. So now it's

Behavior Adjustment. We're on Team B.A., you and I, whether we like it or not, and I can see we'll be on this team quite a while." Armstrong forced a smile. "Let me ask you straight out: are you a Plotter, Dash?"

"Oh, yes. For sure," Dash deadpanned. "I have a secret plan. Meticulously crafted. Be very afraid."

"Would you like to share that plan?"

"Shit, Doc. That was sarcasm. Sorry to frighten you."

"Hear me well, Mr. Askin. If you ever fall in with Plotters, your life will become even more complicated than it is right now. I'd avoid it like the plague. Your freedom can be permanently revoked. I mean that."

"Noted."

"Okay. Let's move on to Six. You remember Six?"

He recited:

Weakness Invites Defeat.

Dash spread his hands in front of him like a magician signaling "voila" with a flourish.

"And do you agree or disagree, Mr. Askin, that weakness invites defeat?"

"I would have to agree with Six, Doc. I really would. It's just self-evident. None of us would want to give up and risk defeat." He turned to face the two-way mirror. "If you're weak, you might as well surrender everything you care about, everything you stand for. Not an option with me. I refuse to be defeated."

"Now, that sounds more like it, Dash," said Armstrong, mistakenly seeing in Dash some miraculous change of heart.

"And Seven. We're making progress."

"Yeah, I love this one, too," Dash lied. In his mind's eye, he could see a statue of wrench-wielding workers sculpted in mid-stride by an artist devoted to Soviet Realism. He recited:

Struggle Is Heroism.

"On second thought, Doc, maybe you can explain this one to me. I'm suddenly drawing a blank."

"Struggle Is Heroism? Think about it, Dash. Everybody has to rise above his permanent economic crisis, right? We all deserve medals just for making it from one day to the next, for rolling up our sleeves and making something out of the rubble of our lives."

"But do you ever wonder, Doc, why it seems the economic crisis is permanent? Why no one ever feels he's making progress? That's fertile ground for a tyrant. The Bosseconomy never really works because if it did, people would be liberated from their grievances."

"Look, we don't have tyrants, Dash, but we do have Plotters. And we've certainly got vermin out there who drain The Bank of Boss by lying around doing nothing. Not to mention what it costs us to round up and Adjust the Behaviors of you and the other DLs. Derangement is a disease, like cancer, Dash. You're afflicted by confusion. But Derangement has a serious public cost. And that's why everyone who can overcome their situation deserves a medal."

"Yeah, apologies for making you struggle, Doc. We gotta conquer this disease, don't we. And if I'm not mistaken, struggle requires manliness, which happens to be Number Eight, right? See, I'm doing your job for you." He recited:

Manliness Is Next to Godliness.

"I memorized that one," Dash said with mock pride. "Absolutely love it."

"Have you ever thought about what it means to be a man, Dash? I mean really thought about it?"

"Like degrading women and forcing them into narrow roles? Not letting women tell you what to do but telling *them* what to do? Being tough, bold, decisive, and never backing down or apologizing?" Dash's rebellious itch was surging. "Like buying a motorcycle and making the muffler really loud? Like refusing to eat sushi or change diapers?"

The clipboard rose. "I'm putting you down as 'Defiant' again."

"Keep your cool, Doc. I'm going for Grudgment Nine." He recited:

Christian Unity Strengthens the People's Voice.

"And I know what it means," Dash beamed. "It means if everyone sings the same hymn at the same time, Jesus and The Boss will be really happy."

"Don't you think our voice as a nation is stronger when we're unified under one banner?" Armstrong asked.

"Jesus is dead, by the way. And that leaves The Boss as the sole embodiment of the People's Voice. I know you think he speaks for everyone..."

"'That's why we hired him, yes. Blessed Be The Boss."

"I hate to clue you in, he doesn't speak for me and he doesn't speak for a lot of other people I know, especially those who don't think our banner should be a single religion, or any religion so distorted it's unrecognizable."

"Well, sir, now I'm putting you down as Belligerent again. And you should be turning in the names of those other people to the Participation Hotline. That's what the law says."

Dash shrugged. "Guilty," he sighed.

"You can recite all the Grudgments," Armstrong said, lost in a moment of clarity, "but you're not understanding why they're necessary. Or you refuse to acknowledge the truth."

"Can't argue with that," Dash said.

"How do we get you to acknowledge the truth?"

Dash's itch was gone, replaced by exasperation, incomprehension, and a grain of defeatism.

"Hate to tell you, Doc, but memorizing The Ten Grudgments is like putting on a blindfold. You don't find anything without your eyes open, especially the truth."

Armstrong, too, was feeling disgusted. "That, sir, is the essence of Derangement."

"Shit, you got me. Can we move on? I'm almost done. Grudgment Ten. Here we go." He recited:

Simple Language, Clearer Thought.

"Now, I'll define clearer thought...."

"Go ahead," Armstrong said, his patience down to the last thread.

"...It means not thinking for yourself, staying dumb enough to keep singing that same hymn without thinking what it means. Keep it simple, black and white, so nobody has to think critically. Nobody even sees the Doublespeak. All reasoning is kicked to the side of the road. Here's something else I memorized years ago, Doctor Armstrong. It goes like this: 'All propaganda must be popular and its intellectual level must be adjusted to the most limited intelligence among those it is addressed to.' Know where that's from? An antique book called *My Struggle*. Well, I guess some people know it by the original German name, *Mein Kampf*. Are you familiar with the author of *Mein Kampf*, Doctor Armstrong?"

The phone rang on Armstrong's desk. He answered and nodded, then uttered one word: "Okay."

The doctor placed the phone on its base and methodically lifted the walkie-talkie attached to his belt. "Two Monitors to 207, please."

Dash smiled. Armstrong smiled back.

"I want you to think hard about what we've discussed here today, Dash. And there's no better place than the Seclusion Room. It's right down the hall. When you're ready to reconsider some of the answers you've given here today, you'll be free to return to Building A and participate in Resource Recovery. So, how long you stay in the Seclusion Room is up to you. Do you understand?"

"Great. I'll have the Continental breakfast and fresh-cut flowers."

Two Monitors with billy clubs and zip ties walked in. Dash rose from the couch and smoothed out his pants. Thick hands gripped each of his upper arms.

"By the way, Mr. Askin" Armstrong added, "visitation is suspended when you're in the Seclusion Room. It's a shame you have to do this to yourself. Polly was looking forward to seeing you. Derangement is painful at first, but it can get better. You'll get through it if you want to. It'll take some work and, as we like to say here, some adjustment."

In less than a minute, Dash was alone inside the Hooch. It was cool, pitch black, silent, and locked. He lay on the padded floor with his hands under his head like a knuckle pillow, staring at a black ceiling that seemed so far away it must have been cut into the floor above. Its surface was dotted with random tiny light bulbs. In the semi-dark, Dash took it to be his personal planetarium. He tried to make out the Big Dipper or Orion's Belt to orient himself, but he couldn't. The bulbs barely illuminated the stainless steel commode in the corner. It was icy to the touch. The Hooch felt like a shadowy clearing under a moonless sky, a void within a greater celestial void. It was the perfect place to think.

4

Polly kept Lily home from school the day Dash was taken away in a straitjacket. They found a couple of nature shows on BTV and baked cookies. Lily cuddled for an hour in Polly's bed before allowing her mother to tuck her in, but neither slept well. Polly replayed every moment of the bizarre hearing in her mind. She was proud of Dash but full of dread about the future — not really for herself and Lily but for Dash.

Lily's subconscious took her to dark places that first night. In her first nightmare, Winston had bitten her dad's calf, and there was blood everywhere. Lily screamed in the dream and woke up moaning. In her second nightmare, Dash was calling to her and she couldn't move her legs. He needed her, but she couldn't reach him.

At breakfast the next morning, Polly tried to learn how traumatized Lily had been by the Sanity Hearing.

"Are you afraid, sweetheart?"

Lily stirred her honeyed cornflakes. "No," she said, seeming to count the individual flakes between yawns.

"It's okay if you are. It's really normal."

"I know."

"Can I tell you something?"

"Okay."

"I'm sort of afraid myself," Polly said.

"You are?" Lily asked, looking up for the first time.

"Of course, I am. It wasn't easy seeing the Enforcers put Daddy in a straitjacket and take him away. It couldn't have been easy for you, either."

"I feel bad because I told Mrs. Ricardo about the rule we have. I didn't mean to, Mommy."

"The you-know-who rule? Not using the name?"

"Mm-hm."

"Do you think Daddy would be here if you hadn't told Mr. Ricardo?"

"Maybe."

"It's not at all true, Lil. They were going to take Daddy the minute they walked in the door with that judge. Nothing would have mattered, sweetie."

"How can they do that?"

"They do it because not enough people speak up to say it's wrong. I knew it might happen one day. Daddy and I talked about it a lot. We told you he was against the regime, and why. Do you remember?"

"Yes."

"But it was still a shock for me to see them take him, and it makes me feel better just to say that, just to be able to talk to you about it."

Polly reached across the table and placed one hand atop Lily's.

"C'm here, li'l peach," she said.

Lily pushed out her chair and walked to the other side of the table with Polly's hand holding her wrist. She put her arms around her mother's neck and her cheek against her warm face. They held each other.

"He'll be okay, Mommy," Lily whispered. "You told me we have to show Daddy we're going to be okay."

"We will, peach."

The catharsis reverberated through both of them. Polly put Lily on her lap and held her close. She stroked Lily's hair for a long time. Lily couldn't help thinking of separation: Polly's separation from Dash and Lily's separation from the feeling of safety that her dad always gave her. When Polly composed herself, she looked at her daughter, and asked: "Did you know that when you were about to go into kindergarten, Daddy and I thought we might send you to private school?"

"Why?"

"Because we wanted to protect you from the worst of Bossism. At least that was our instinct. That was our hope."

"Daddy always calls it the Poison of Bossism. But why am I in public school, then?"

"Because we knew that no matter how hard we worked to protect you, Bossism would be everywhere — on the Internet, on your phone, in conversations with your friends. We didn't want you to think there were two different worlds, one safe from Bossism and one full of Bossism — full of ..." Polly was thinking of the distorted rhetoric, the bullying and intimidation, the grievance, the ignorance, the propaganda, the thought control, the prying, even the brutality, but she held back. "...full of the bad things about Bossism. There's not another world where it's safe and you can forget. It's not something you just hide from. It's not good to hide from other people's suffering. You stop caring. Do you remember what Daddy said about democracy?"

"It's an idea from the past that people forgot about."

"Yes, and somebody has to keep it alive."

"Like Daddy?"

"Yes, like Daddy. And like a lot of people in the Sanctuaries. But many people who want to keep the idea of democracy alive aren't in Sanctuaries. Like me. And like you, and all the people who are just starting their lives."

"But we're kids. What can kids do?"

"Well, you're growing up and you can make a difference in the world. Every generation leaves its mark, positive or negative, and the next generation either benefits or suffers. It's why we don't let you watch too much BTV alone, why we watch together so we can talk about what you see. We sent you to public school, but we've also done a lot of home-schooling, haven't we."

"Yes."

"Do you see, peach? We want you to have the tools to think for yourself and not just do whatever people tell you, or think the way other people think, whatever your friends say or even your teachers."

"Daddy told me not to tell you, but he used a B word. He said he wanted me to know bullshit when I see it."

Polly laughed. "Do you understand what he means?"

"Yeah. Daddy said you-know-who wants us to be afraid of other people who aren't like us so he can pretend to protect us."

"Do you think it might be better if people trusted each other and cared about each other and helped each other?"

"Yes."

"That's the kind of world Daddy is trying to bring back. But it's hard."

Polly and Dash didn't place all the responsibility for Bossism on Acton Grudge. As parents, they also tried to teach Lily that when it comes to political leadership, people sometimes hand over their own power too willingly, follow the crowd without thinking, accept at face value what their leader tells them, or just give up and tune everything out.

"I wish you could have met your other grandparents," Polly said. "Papa and Nanna would have loved seeing you grow up, and I'm pretty sure they would have helped you understand why Bossism hurts all of us and why we have to try to change it."

Dash and Polly had raised Lily with the hope that, one day, things would change and she would need to be prepared for that change — maybe even be a person who could bring about the change. They bought bootleg copies of banned children's books with messages rooted in bygone values like courage, respect, and trust. They bought black market flash drives holding banned multiracial educational videos and secretly swapped them with other families who were doing the same. They hid all of them in a cabinet carved out of a wall and disguised as wood paneling.

"Do you know why we got Winston, honey?" Polly asked.

"I love Winston."

"I know. We all love him. We wanted to teach you love and care and empathy and patience."

"I think you did."

"But you have to care for people the way you care for Winston, right? Do you think Winston loves you?"

"I know he does. He told me."

They both laughed.

"And you know why we have a family vote before planning a trip?"

"I forget."

"Democracy. Everyone has a voice. Everyone has power."

"I knew that. But it's gone, right?"

"Right."

"I like when we talk about what to make for dinner and then vote."

"We have a debate, don't we."

"Yeah. That's fun. Salad against meatballs."

"It's hard to do with just two people, but when Daddy's back, we'll do it again."

"Mommy, are you sure Daddy will come back?"

"Yes. But we have to be patient."

"Will democracy come back?"

"If we don't forget it. If we don't just say, 'Well, this is the way it's going to be, so why bother.' Those people are the Passivists, and the Passivists would rather not think about what's really wrong in society and how to make it better."

"Do most people even know what democracy is? My friends don't."

"I think more people know than talk about it. They're just afraid to talk about it, Lil. They're afraid of informants and afraid of the regime."

"Like the snitchers?"

"Yes, the snitchers. And they're afraid you-know-who might punish them."

"When can we see Daddy? I want him to know we're not afraid."

Polly paused before replying. Her daughter seemed more mature and aware about what had happened than she'd thought. It was a relief. Polly tried not to soft-soap the truth with Lily about Dash's situation. One thing was out of bounds, though: his sabotage inside CompuLink. If he were ever caught, she knew he was as good as dead.

"Next weekend. Maybe. But I want you to know it might be difficult."

"I'll be okay, Mom."

"You might see Enforcers and high walls and barbed wire and bars on the windows. A Sanctuary is a strange place. They never existed before Bossism. People inside aren't sick, you know. Dad's not sick. You-know-who just wants to put them away so they'll stop working against him. They make up a sickness, Derangement. It's not real."

"I know."

"The regime is afraid of the people in the Sanctuaries, so they take away their freedom and try to change their minds."

"Do you think Daddy will stop working against you-know-who?"

"He never will, Lily. I can almost guarantee that. It's just something he has to do."

"But will they hurt Daddy like they did to Papa and Nanna?"

"Honey, it's so hard to know. I hope not. Your Dad is a very brave man. Braver than I can ever explain. I'm not even sure how he can be so brave. But you have to understand that he can take care of himself, and he's never going to give up what he believes or pretend he believes something else."

"I'm just worried about him. I'm not really afraid for myself, but I'm worried about Daddy. Do you know what I mean?"

"Of course, honey. We can both be worried. It's good to be a little bit worried. But we should try not to be afraid when we visit him. He needs to see that we're doing fine. We are, aren't we?"

"I think so."

"It's okay if we tell him we're worried. It shows we care. But we want him to know that we're strong and ready to face whatever happens, and we believe in him. Do you think you can do that, Lil?"

"I think so."

"I know you can."

"I will."

Dash wasn't without social skills growing up, but he was far more comfortable inside his own mind as a boy, considering how things worked, why rocks fell and feathers drifted, how birds stayed aloft, why stars came out at night, why snow evaporated even in the cold, how fish lived underwater. Mike and Katharine came to believe they had a scientist in the making, and they agreed that he took after his dad, the climate ecologist. The books Dash loved most were about dinosaurs, astronomy, deep sea creatures, and space. Then he graduated to young adult novels about adventurers and explorers. He left the book about famous Presidents untouched. Dash loved numbers from an exceptionally early age and couldn't get enough when Mike peppered him with math problems while riding in the back seat of the car. His parents began to see a competitive streak in Dash and a determination to solve problems of all kinds, from a stuck zipper to algebraic equations. Dash didn't like giving up.

By the time he entered middle school, he was mastering every chemistry set his parents could put in front of him, and he'd learned how to write basic computer code in two different programming languages. But Dash also became so headstrong at school that he would occasionally challenge his teachers when he thought they were oversimplifying or missing essential elements of an explanation. This posed a dilemma for his parents. They delighted in their son's insistence on exactitude and working a problem to its successful completion and speaking his mind. They even quietly sympathized when, at a parent-teacher conference, his math teacher gently explained that Dash's challenges in class were bordering on disrespect and arrogance.

Katharine and Mike preferred to think of it as a healthy rebelliousness. But they saw its potential to bring Dash grief, so they started talking to him about humility and acknowledging the experience of adults. They were careful not to instill or give license to servility or acquiescence, however. It was a fine line, and if it had to be crossed, they wanted Dash never to feel he needed to defer to others whose ideas violated the values they were trying to teach him.

The lesson was seared into his heart soon before his fifteenth birthday when BBI agents raided the Askin home, handcuffed Mike and Katharine, and took them to jail. At that moment, politics was thrust into Dash's world like a tornado, and it didn't take long for the social implications of power politics to become an obsession.

When Dash first met Polly, he worried about how to explain all of this. They encountered each other at CompuLink during a Red Cross employee training session on the use of portable defibrillators. Dash laughed out loud when Polly complained that the plastic dummy wasn't even close to lifelike.

"It's a robot," Polly joked, "and they don't have hearts, so why are we here?"

He learned that Polly was an artist and worked in Marketing, but all Dash knew for sure was that she was a work of art. He hesitated over the concept of marketing, which he wasn't sure he understood. Wasn't marketing something like propaganda? Selling stuff that couldn't sell itself? Convincing people they needed something they didn't really need? Creating vague affinity groups? Mostly, though, he worried about pursuing a relationship if the two of them turned out to be on opposite sides of the Great Political Divide. This was one of Bossism's supreme irritants: how to know whether a person you meet will one day call the Participation Hotline and brand you a Deranged dissident who isn't properly falling into line in The Boss's parade of subservience.

It was on their second date that Polly took the initiative, thus relieving Dash of the responsibility for finding out if they held opposite opinions of The Boss.

"What do you think of the people at CompuLink?" she asked casually as they sat on a shaded park bench on a hot Sunday afternoon in June.

"I get along with most of them. Engineers and computer scientists don't always have sparkling personalities, though. Except for me, of course."

"I notice you don't sparkle very much in the cafeteria. You eat alone. Are you lost in your work, or trying to avoid sitting down with people and talking about the elephant in the room?"

Dash laughed. "The Big Elephant, yeah. And all the other circus animals."

"Where there's a zoo, there are animals, right?"

Dash asked: "Are we talking about biology or politics?"

"Sometimes, I think they're the same. Anyway, no. I meant the biggest of the B words."

"Bossism."

"Yes. Bossism."

The door was wide open and Dash leaped through. "I have to tell you, I'm an A-1 Boss Hater. Been that way for a long, long time."

"Oh, thank God!" Polly exulted. "So am I."

For hours that afternoon, they psychoanalyzed The Boss while strolling along the edge of the park in a zig-zag pattern to avoid the ubiquitous pole-mounted security cameras. Dash suspected many were decoys, empty pieces of plastic tacked up high at random to make everyone think they were being watched from above. It was less expensive than actually watching. That was the difference between Chinese and American methods of mind control. China used the terror of the gun liberally and wanted everyone to know it. The Boss preferred a mix of quiet, targeted terror and fake mass-market benevolence.

As they walked, Dash and Polly reviewed the more nauseating tendencies of the regime, commiserated over the split with Pacifica, and tried to unravel the weird psychology of it all — why so many people relinquished their own agency and acceded to The Boss's absurd demands. Dash would have gone on for hours about the corruption, the ignorance, and the influence of the Boss Billionaires, but he didn't. He felt relieved just to have met a woman who might understand his deep need to oppose Bossism.

Eventually, he would need to tell Polly the whole truth about his life with Katharine and Mike. All she knew was that both of his parents had died a couple of weeks apart when Dash was in his teens. It took him two months to find the right moment to tell Polly about his unusual upbringing.

During a dinner out, he explained everything in whispers and napkin diagrams. "My parents were both professors. My mom taught Ancient Philosophy and my dad was an engineer and taught Climate Ecology," Dash told her. "You have to understand, when Bossism took over, they became real rebels, I mean dedicated insurgents, and they paid a price."

"What do you mean?"

"They were in the thick of the protests all over the country around the time of the first Big Burn. The Boss was young and feeling like he could conquer anything. My parents tried to keep a low profile, but that didn't last very long. Eventually, the BBI caught on, and they were arrested. The agents raided our house and took away a bunch of banned books. I had to go live with my aunt. She took me to see them in jail."

"Oh, Dash."

"I'll never forget it. They were in for just sixty days, but during that time both of their departments at the university were axed. The Boss was cutting off funding to any institution he thought was a breeding ground for Boss Hate, and the universities were cowering. So, they lost their jobs."

"You must have been terrified."

"It was pretty hard. My aunt took me to a therapist because I guess I was depressed. At first, I thought my parents had abandoned me or at least didn't care what happened to me. I was pretty angry. When they got out, things improved because they explained to me how deeply they felt that Bossism was a disaster and would get worse unless people tried to stop it. It was my introduction to politics. Dad made me realize that it mattered. I remember his exact words. He told me, 'Politics is the distribution of power from those with the means to *take* power to those so weakened they have to meet the taker's demands.' All of a sudden, I could see that hiding in the world of science was a bit artificial. Why make better software when people are losing their freedom, their ability to control their very lives?"

"It's a lot to take in," Polly said. "What happened to them, Dash?"

"'There was a period of calm after they got out of jail. Mom and Dad tried to prepare me by telling me they couldn't just shut off their defiance of the regime. It was in their genes. They started organizing protests again. One was against The Boss's decree forcing everyone to pay dues to the League of Christian Voters, even non-Christians. Both of them were jailed again. It was inevitable. They knew it would happen, but they did it anyway. They explained everything to me. I couldn't imagine such courage, but I started to feel afraid for them. I admired what they were doing. How couldn't I? But it was so dangerous. After a while, I realized I'd inherited their defiance. I could feel it."

"You have a lot of amazing traits, and I'm beginning to see why," Polly said.

"They went to prison for a year, Pol. Not just jail. Prison. I started high school at my aunt's. When they got out, I thought maybe things would return to normal. Instead, it got very nasty. The BBI followed them. Mom and Dad told me our phones were tapped. They told me not to talk about certain things at home or on the phone. We took walks a lot so we could speak freely. They were already felons, but they couldn't stop. They refused to stop. They joined a group of a hundred or so other academics who were about to create something called Teachers Against Big Brotherism."

"Oh, God, I remember the trial, now. Was that your parents?"

"Yeah. As soon as they announced the group, the BBI agents showed up again and a swarm of them turned the house upside down. They took cartons of personal stuff. Computers. Everything. I was at school, but I saw what they'd done when I got home."

"Everybody was charged with treason, right?"

"Treason, seditious conspiracy, and, in the case of my parents, espionage. A hundred people. The Boss went completely nuts about that trial. He wanted a big show on BTV, so there was an elaborate trial."

"I remember it ran every day for weeks, didn't it? But I was at school."

"The Boss's people brought in a ton of witnesses, ex-colleagues and friends of all these professors, who swore they'd heard every one of them conspiring to use violence. Except no one had a recording. It was all hearsay. They had no intention of turning to violence. And all the witnesses against them received Participation Payments for so-called 'time and trouble,' and you never knew how much."

"I'm afraid to ask what happened."

"They had big parts in that courtroom drama. My uncle Ben, Dad's brother, lied to the BBI. He made a fortune selling air-conditioners. Then he turned to short-selling the euro during the Petro-Currency Crisis. I don't know if that blinded him somehow, or if the regime threatened to take away all his wealth if he didn't cooperate. Anyway, Ben provided plenty of juicy testimony. None of it was true, but all of it sounded damning, shocking even. He lied about everything. Testified that Mike and Katharine told him that Chinese agents had paid them to plant a bomb inside the Department of Modern Creationism at the university. This is his brother and his sister-in-law, remember. It was awful. No money ever showed up in their personal accounts, but the jury took twenty minutes to convict them. Ben went underground. I haven't seen him since, and I still don't know what he got out of turning my parents in. It's a good thing I haven't seen him, because if I did, I'd probably kill him with my bare hands."

Polly had her hand over her mouth. Dash was trying to keep his emotions in check. He steadied his voice.

"Mom and Dad were shipped to different maximum-security prisons. I couldn't visit them very often. Every two months. It didn't take the goons long to shut my dad up for good. The story the regime told was that he had some health problem and died in the prison hospital, but Dad was fifty-seven and healthy. It just didn't make sense. The warden had a hard time explaining it without embarrassing himself. All kinds of contradictions. I'm pretty sure they poisoned him."

Polly's eyes were brimming, and she couldn't speak.

"Katharine died a week later at another prison. Both autopsies said 'natural causes.' The Boss needed to make examples of them, to tamp down copycat martyrs. They probably poisoned Mom, too, or maybe she died of a broken heart when she learned Dad was gone. Nobody ever gave me any explanation. The prison refused to release the autopsies. This is what I mean by targeted terror. Never underestimate the brutal instincts of the regime, no matter how much they cloak themselves in Christianity."

"What a trauma for you," Polly said. "How did you go on?"

"It's ironic, but I think my last visit to my Dad gave me a lot of willpower. We were in the visitor room at the prison, and he apologized. He just said, 'I'm sorry, Dash.' And I asked him, 'For what?' And he said 'For leaving you. For not protecting you. For everything.' I told him he and Mom had done the right thing. And he said 'Yeah, but it's hopeless, Dashy boy.' I'll never forget those words. He told me it's hopeless, all this struggle for a better world, for justice. That's what they believed in. You know, I was actually a little angry at him. I told him 'No, it's not hopeless.' And he said, 'Have a life, son. Don't be like me. It's a waste.' I was so sad about that, and I really can't let that image go."

Dash could tell Polly's heart was breaking. He wanted her to care. He needed her to understand.

"I think I was programmed to ignore Dad's advice," he continued. "I knew I'd never give up trying to achieve what they were trying to achieve. That's what's inside me, Polly. If you're going to be with me, you just have to understand why I'm the way I am. One day, it'll be my turn. I don't know when or how, but I can feel it. Call it fate or whatever you want, but one day I might be in the same place they were, in a Sanctuary or a penitentiary. I want you to think about it. You have to imagine it, Pol. Because I may not be the guy you want to stay with."

What Polly heard from Dash about his parents frightened her. There was no love of Bossism in her own family, but their opposition was muted, as if her parents had simply decided to live with an unsatisfactory situation — not hardcore Passivism, but close. She was drawn to art her entire life, and it became a refuge as she realized how much Bossism was affecting her. In her soul, she was an empathetic and completely open person. Open to people, open to ideas, open to experience. But Bossism had cast a cloud of wariness over her life, and she hated what it did to her. The Boss's efforts to manipulate information and encourage informants disgusted her. She hated having to wonder if the person she was talking to might turn her in to the BBI. She didn't know which of her co-workers and acquaintances she could trust. She yearned to be her genuine self, but she found that the implications of Bossism, its reliance on intimidation and blind loyalty, colored nearly all of her relationships.

She worried that Dash might do something rash to pursue revenge for his parents' deaths.

"It's awful, for sure, Dash. But how badly do you want to harm them? I mean, how intolerable are they to you?"

"I'm not an impulsive person, Pol."

"But you try to wrestle every problem to the ground."

"Maybe I do, but are you saying I shouldn't?"

"I'm just saying I don't want to lose you — the beautiful you — to a demon inside you."

"There's no demon. I've thought about this, Pol. So many people sign on to the Passivist philosophy. Are we supposed to watch from the sidelines while things get worse? I can't do that. Someone has to push back. In areas where I can make a difference, isn't it my duty to try?"

"I can't argue with that, it's just...."

"You're afraid."

"Yes."

"I'm sorry. The truth is, so am I. I don't do many things blindly. I try to think them through. And sometimes I just feel that risks are inevitable. I don't want to lose you, either, Pol. I can't deny who I am."

"How do you feel about raising children under Bossism?"

"There was a time, in my late teens, when my anger was so strong that I thought it might consume me. I couldn't have imagined raising kids under Bossism. I think I've outgrown that. I've matured. I hope you'd be okay with raising kids today, because in a way it affirms what's good about life, and you have a chance to mold someone and teach them why Passivism is the wrong path — even with schools that proselytize Prayer, Order, Security and Shut-up-ism. I want my kids to respect everyone, to think for themselves, and to be independent in a crazy world where fear drives everything."

That was the moment Polly truly fell in love with Dash. She felt he could see right inside her soul, that he had spoken the words in her heart.

Polly gave birth two years after the wedding. Those were happy years but not necessarily easy ones. They led a careful life. They wanted to be aware and purposeful, even in the face of a repellant political environment. The topic they wrestled with most was how best to educate Lily.

Under Bossism, billions in public money poured effortlessly into parental vouchers that allowed the Christian School industry to boom. There were even outright grants by the regime to the new Values Schools, which were essentially driven by the same thought-control techniques used by the regime. The public schools that survived operated as hybrid institutions. They became places where prayer participation was mandatory but spoken prayers were optional. Uniforms became the norm, but sneakers of any kind were acceptable. Metal detectors and biometrics were routinely deployed for security, except for the weapons locked in every teacher's desk. The definition of Shut-up-ism evolved to cover many more books and music recordings on the banned lists, and some topics of conversation in the schools became grounds for suspension — anything related to sexuality, any criticism of the regime that wasn't deemed "constructive," and any concepts of world or American history that deviated from the Boss-mandated curriculum.

The Values Schools were far stricter. Classes in Prayer and Christian Studies were mandatory, as were Riflery, History as Glory, Clean English, Flag Care, Decent Role Models, and Behavior Adjustment.

In the evenings and on weekends, Polly and Dash read what they called Special Books to Lily, ones they thought would help counteract the worst elements of the Bossism creed. Each had a message, like tolerance, respect, or how to listen. Some were biographies of pioneers in thought, science, or justice. Some were poetry books. Each was removed from the secret cabinet and returned with the same care one might reserve for a family heirloom.

When Lily was ten, Dash and Polly sat her down and explained the real circumstances of his parents' deaths. She seemed confused at first and asked a lot of questions, hard ones. Winston was there, and they did their best to help her grapple with the darker impulses of the world. Dash was gently forthright during that conversation, but he lied to Lily about one thing. He told her that Nanna and Papa had always told Dash that nothing was hopeless and to never give up.

"Okay, Daddy," Lily said. "I won't give up." In her heart, though, she didn't know if she could live up to that promise.

"That's good, peach," Dash said as he held Lily in his arms. "Because if you give up, it's like putting your brain on automatic. You don't have to think for yourself ever again."

5

In the meditative darkness of the Seclusion Room, Dash channeled LeBeau's prescription for surviving the Hooch and placed himself in a zen-like state by humming "Amazing Grace" in a languid loop. His mind traveled two paths. The first propelled him toward a deeper realization of his good fortune in having a family that understood him and believed in him, despite the dangers. The second pulled him to a place of pragmatic calculation: how to exit Solitary with his self-respect intact so he could help fire up the Underground.

Dash understood The Boss's goal all too well: to corrode his resistance and eventually return him to society as a productive cipher, a worthy yet weightless person, floating through life without influence or purpose or responsibility beyond programming for CMI by day to keep the lights on at home and watching ball games at night with a sweaty bottle of BossBeer in his hand. This was the ticket Dr. Armstrong was offering.

In a sense, this is what The Boss wanted for everyone. Dash believed The Boss's obsession was to oversee an unquestioning colony of sheep who relinquished their individual values and voices in return for security and order. The Boss offered relief from the burdens of citizenship and the difficult work democracy required. He saw himself as the essential shepherd, guiding a flock of Passivists who would remain content with a predictable life where everyone who watched BTV understood the rules and shut up about the rest. The Boss relied on citizens who knew the Bosseconomy would provide the minimum needed for a good life: an air-conditioned home with a pickup truck in the driveway, affordable gasoline prices, the unqualified right to firearms, schools with a late-pickup program, occasional wrestling tickets, plentiful burgers, Halcitol, and a dog.

Reluctantly, Dash acknowledged that the deal was attractive for many people. When they felt they'd been dealt a "Life's a Bitch" card, here came The Boss with an unbeatable option: we'll tear up the "Life's a Bitch" card and hand you three new ones, "Let *Me* Deal With *Them*," "Good Shut-up-ism Makes Good Neighbors," and "Be Happy on Halcitol."

Dash preferred the "Life's a Bitch" card if it allowed him to pursue his own convictions with the freedom to think and dream, and with a belief that nothing is hopeless. He asked himself if he was stubbornly trying to avenge the murder of his parents and decided their memory deserved more than a footnote and their killers less than mercy. His motivation went far beyond his family's honor, though. His soul yearned for autonomy and freedom from fear. Dash believed that Bossism's meaningless dominance over society — control for control's sake — deserved a death as brutal as the methods it required to exert its will. He longed to sink his jaw into The Boss's fat ankle like a rabid dog and to hold on.

But you can't do that from inside the Seclusion Room. Dash wanted to brainstorm with LeBeau and the others, to put his computer skills to work and to somehow restore communications with the other Sanctuaries — to make the Underground live up to the reason it existed. Getting back to Building **A** would require swallowing hard and playing

The Boss's game with as much cleverness as he could summon.

He pushed the red button on the intercom near the Seclusion Room door.

When the Monitors delivered Dash to Room 207, Dr. Richard Armstrong looked hesitant but seemed prepared to compromise. Armstrong truly believed that Derangement was an illness brought on by anger, stubbornness, and a misguided yearning for a Godless Utopia that was impractical and morally empty.

"Well, Dash, I'm certainly glad to see you. Have you had a chance to think things through?"

Dash peered down at the floor with an air of remorse and hangdog misery. "We got off on the wrong foot, so I'd like to review The Ten Grudgments again. You know, take another shot."

"I see. I see," Armstrong replied, measuring the depth of Dash's sincerity. "And why is that?"

"It's not as if *all* The Ten Grudgments appeal to me, Doc. But I think I can get my head around some of them. Anyway, I'm willing to rethink it. To be honest, I don't much like the view from the Seclusion Room. I guess you knew that. But it gave me a chance to think more about what you said."

"So, you feel some motivation?"

"Yes, motivation. I want to see my wife and daughter and try to leave Sanctuary Thirteen as soon as I've served my time," he lied. "It's nice enough here, but it's not meant to be for the long haul."

"That's all well and good, but why should I believe you're committed to conquering your own Derangement?" Armstrong asked. "You can't pretend to take The Ten Grudgments to heart, you know, just to go back home and pick up where you left off, harboring all that Lunatic anger and bile."

"I just think it's worth starting the process, to see if I can make progress," Dash lied before shifting into truth mode: "I'd be lying if I told you I think I can free myself from Derangement in a few weeks and go back home a happy man."

"Well, then, it seems like we should give it a go," Armstrong concluded. "Provisionally, of course. I do reserve the right to recommend a longer sentence, or even to send you back to the Seclusion Room if things don't go well. You're going to have to come at this with an open mind and an open heart, Dash. Derangement can be awful, but it can be cured. I like to incorporate prayer, too. How do you feel about prayer, Dash?"

"I guess I tried it as a kid, but I left it on the sidelines. You know, life takes over."

"Well, I'm gonna let you go back. It being Sunday, I think you can have Polly come up to see you this afternoon, if she can make it, but I first want you to get your Halcitol shot and attend Chapel. God hears all prayers, Dash, even ones from Jews."

"That's very comforting," Dash lied as he exited Behavioral Health, determined to secretly unleash a searing Royal Fucking upon The Boss. He was almost as eager to talk to LeBeau about his plan as he was to see his wife and daughter.

T he gateposts and walls that Polly and Lily drove past to reach Sanctuary Thirteen were topped with barbed wire, and black-clad Monitors stood out front on a gravel path strewn with red and orange leaves liberated by the early November breezes. If the place disturbed Lily, as

Polly had feared, her daughter didn't let on. Polly's mission was to assess Dash's condition and mental state. Lily's mission was to deliver a message to her father.

The Monitors searched them just inside Building A with a detector wand and allotted thirty minutes in the Community Room with Dash. There were other visitors that day, huddled in clutches about the room. Dash had a fresh Halcitol shot in his system, a requirement whenever visitors were expected. LeBeau called it the "put on a happy face injection." When Dash explained Halcitol to Polly — "it's just like an antidepressant" — her heart sank and she struggled to avoid showing it. Lily was confused but said nothing, because she could see her dad looked well and his voice was strong. Polly, too, saw that the person on the couch with her was focused, intelligent, expressive, and courageous, just like the man she'd known right through the Derangement Hearing. Still, she felt anxious and wary. She asked if he was eating okay.

"It's wall-to-wall burgers, but I'm surviving. I eat a big breakfast and try to avoid beef at other meals. It's times like this that I feel starved for lettuce and avocados. I can't wait for the border with Pacifica to reopen."

"Are there people you can talk to?" Polly asked.

"Are you kidding? I'm still meeting them, but there are amazing people here — ex-military officers, journalists, writers, scientists, artists, and regular people who just decided they had to take a stand. They call themselves the Nobody's. I can't give you names — it's not allowed."

"Is the staff treating you alright?"

"They're superficially friendly, and very watchful."

Dash could see the worry on Polly's face. He took her hands.

"You know the worst thing they try to do to you in here, Pol? They try to convert you to Bossism and The Ten Grudgments. But that's what they do *outside* these walls, too. Re-education. Thought police. It's the same. I've lived with that my whole life and almost find it amusing. You've lived with it, too. So don't worry about me. It's a waste of your time and energy. I'm going to use my time here wisely."

"How so?"

"I just mean I'm not going to waste away. Despite the Halcitol, my brain is intact and my motivation hasn't drained away. I have to work in the salvage plant, without pay, but during Exercise Hour and in the evenings, even during Chapel, I think about ways to be relevant."

"Relevant? Is something going on?"

"No, honey."

"Relevant to what?"

"Nothing, Pol. Nothing I can talk about, anyway."

It was Dash's way of signaling that something was up. Polly knew he was scheming, planning, and probably conspiring. This was her husband. She was frightened for him, but she was also relieved. He was showing her he hadn't lost any of his purpose.

"Be careful. Please be careful," she whispered to him.

"You know I will."

"And you'll let me know if you need anything or need me to do anything?"

"I'm glad you asked. I do need something. Next visit, can you bring me a book? It's not banned yet, but it's big and it's going to be expensive so try to buy it used. I need *The Yale Complete Works of Shakespeare*."

She could see in Dash's eyes that it wasn't sonnets he was after.

Lily had been listening quietly but also surveying the other DLs, the visitors, the attendants, and the Monitors around the Community Room. She turned to Dash.

"Daddy, they seem like normal people here."

"Normal? Ah, sweetheart. All the DLs are people like me. Some of them had pretty important jobs, even inside the regime, and others are just regular people with guts. They're smart, and I like them." He lowered his voice and leaned toward her. "But everything is upside down and inside out here, Lil. We're supposedly the Deranged Lunatics threatening all the sane people. The staff thinks we can't see reality. They think you-know-who is harmless. If I said to them we're the actual prisoners and they're all brainwashed, they'd send me straight to the medical office."

"It sounds upside down and inside out, kind of like *Alice in Wonderland*, where..."

Dash finished her sentence: "....where the Queen of Hearts wants to cut off everyone's head? Yes. Like that."

"But Alice wakes up."

"I wish this was just a bad dream, peach. But no one is going to cut off my head. It's screwed on pretty tight."

Polly winced at the harsh image. Lily was quiet for a moment.

"Daddy, do they try to hurt you in here? I mean, do they do what that judge did?"

"You mean threaten me?"

"Uh-huh. Do they force you to do stuff you don't want to do?"

Dash shook his head and smiled at her.

"No one is going to hurt me, li'l peach. Do you see that I'm the same me?"

"I guess. But you have to be careful."

"You know I will."

Lily was lost in thought for a moment. Suddenly she blurted: "Daddy, don't give up, no matter what, okay? I promise I won't, and you have to promise you won't."

Startled, Polly and Dash looked at each other before Dash turned back to his daughter.

"I won't give up, sweetheart," Dash whispered. "And I'm so proud of you right now. I know you won't give up, either."

"Promise?" she whispered.

"I promise."

When their time was up, Polly rose and embraced her husband, found his ear and said quietly: "Listen to your daughter, Dash. Just be very careful."

L eBeau wrapped a brotherly arm around Dash's shoulders when he returned to their room.

"Where you been? The Hooch?"

Dash smiled. "They offered me a discount if I stayed three nights."

"When I was in for a week, I won two extra nights for swearing at them with some pretty ugly language. So I dialed it back and just called them fuckin' bastards. It was good."

Dash told LeBeau about his visit with Polly, then recalled how he'd told Armstrong to shove The Ten Grudgments before being tossed into the Hooch. They laughed, but LeBeau knew Armstrong hadn't sprung Dash from the Seclusion Room out of the goodness of his heart. Dash must have done or said something to get himself back to Building A so quickly. Later, during the Sunday afternoon Exercise Hour, LeBeau tried to squeeze the real story from Dash. They re-enacted their workout routine and exchanged banter between sit-ups. The basic story he heard was that Dash realized you can't accomplish anything meaningful sitting inside the blackened Seclusion Room.

"I need to feel my time inside Thirteen will amount to something," Dash told LeBeau. "I don't want to just say Grace morning and night, pull wires out of voting machines, kiss Armstrong's ass, and scratch days off the calendar. If there was no Underground, I'd probably start one. But there *is* an Underground, and I need to be part of it. Do you get that, LeBeau? Spending time in the Hooch is a waste."

LeBeau almost felt sorry for Dash. "We'll get you going. Don't worry about that. But at the moment there's a big problem. Until we replace our secret phone somehow, or find another way to connect to the Web, we're basically on the far side of the Moon. We don't know what other Sanctuaries are doing. They don't know what we're doing. We can't get beyond these walls."

"I've been thinking about that," Dash said.

"Yeah, so have I, but I'm coming up empty. Caleb's job is to get us another phone, but he's not optimistic. They don't know he got us the first one, but they're checking all the staff every day. They're doing metal-detector walk-throughs and random searches. He's shittin' bricks. So, basically, we're dead in the water."

Dash stopped LeBeau. "What if I told you we might be able to build our own communications device? I mean, not a real phone that could make calls. But something with a mobile browser that could at least get us to the Web. Like a mini-computer."

LeBeau laughed. "I'd say you're either the most deranged fuckin' DL on the planet or on a triple dose of Halcitol."

"No, I mean it. I checked the library and found an article in *Popular Mechanics* on how to build your own mobile phone. It's right under their noses."

"You're hallucinating."

Dash was losing his patience. "I'm not hallucinating, LeBeau. I'm a fucking engineer. A damned good one. I studied this shit. I may need some help, but I know we can find enough components inside the Resource Recovery Center — steal the parts we need — and build a crude device. Just something simple with the functions we need. I'm fucking serious. Don't tell me it can't be done."

"Alright. Alright. I'm listening, okay? Tell me the plan."

"Fine. I need special metals, plastics, and wiring to produce a crude System on a Chip. I need memory components and a makeshift camera lens. I want to produce fake documents, so I need something to take photos of them so they can be uploaded to the Web."

"Okay. You've got my attention."

"I need to make a device with a modem and a simple black and white display just to transmit documents. The device would probably have to be double the size of our mobile phones. I can't really miniaturize anything unless there are chipsets on the salvage plant assembly line."

"Shit, there *are* chipsets."

"I figured there were. We'd build each component separately. Work at night and find hiding places. I have ideas about that. If we can build and test each component, we could put them together in the final stage."

"How long do you think it would take?"

"After I have the parts, I'd need maybe two or three weeks. It depends on how much time I can find to do the work. There's one essential item I'm pretty sure we can't make, though."

"Which is?"

"The battery."

"Right. The fucking battery. Maybe Caleb could get us one. It would be a lot easier than smuggling in a whole phone. He should be able to come up with some excuse for putting one through the metal detector. You're serious about this, aren't you."

"I think I can do this, LeBeau. I mean, shouldn't we try?"

"We've got nothing to lose. Let me talk to some people in here who know their way around the salvage plant and figure out if we can walk out with the stuff you need in our pockets. We'd have to study security to look for gaps."

They ran through exercises along the path, talking between grunts.

"There's a lot of risk in doing something like this," LeBeau said. "Not everyone'll wanna give us a hand. What's the reward? I mean, sure, we restore communication with the Underground, but I need to motivate people if we're gonna ask them to smuggle components from the salvage plant. It's risky. They need to see a tangible goal, something they can tell their grandkids they helped accomplish when push came to shove. So what's the goal? What's the FTB you're thinking about?"

"A Royal Fucking. Stay with me. We know The Boss's mindset. We know his frailties and his fears. We know the image he has to keep burnished for so many people to fall for his act. We know his facade means everything. So what if we could plant damaging information in the public arena that sounded like it *could* be true — shocking information about The Boss and the regime that'll raise suspicions, information that would seep up from the Dark Web into the social media swamp. With any luck, the stuff we plant would cause cracks in the fake world he's so carefully built. We want people to question if he's real or fake, if he's telling the truth or conning them. At the very least, it would drive The Boss up the fucking wall."

"So, these fake documents would have to be believable, right? Shocking but believable. Is that it?"

"Exactly. We create credible-looking papers inside Thirteen and upload them to the Web. I know we can make authentic-looking documents. They'd have to look like they came right from The Boss's safe or were leaked by someone close to him. I want him to get paranoid. If I can make this new device work the way I think I can, we'd take pictures of the docs and just upload them to a few key places. The Boss traffics in disinformation all the time, but we can fight back with our own. Their disinformation versus ours. You see?"

"I get the concept. Whaddaya think is going to have the most punch?"

"Here's an example. What if we could post a fake prescription with The Boss's name on it that shows he has some kind of medical issue he's trying to hide."

"Like what?"

"Erectile dysfunction."

"Oh. Now I get it. If a prescription looks real, he'll be mighty pissed off. He'd have to deny it. When he does, the story gets amplified."

"You see? We could do half a dozen of those. I need some more ideas. I thought I'd talk to the Brain Trust and get a list together."

Dash gradually posed intriguing questions to the Brain Trust in private corners of Building A. If we want to create Royal Fuckings that are sure to get under The Boss's skin, which of his vulnerabilities should we attack? What scandalous documents can we drop onto the Dark Web that will have a chance of exploding onto social media because they seem credible? Can we sow mistrust and dissension among The Boss, his staff, and the Boss Billionaires he depends on?

Dash came up with a few answers of his own, but the best emerged from Max Willen, the public health psychiatrist, and Eleanor Ruby, the Hollywood screenwriter. Together, they had an uncanny ability to see The Boss's foibles and imagine ways to poke him to the point that he felt unloved and paranoid.

Max asked, "He's leading this crusade of White people, right? What if it turns out he's not all White?"

Eleanor went to work imagining fake documents that would goad, prod, frighten, or embarrass. She sketched out official-looking government spreadsheets, invoices, memoranda, and pharmacy prescriptions, all with the requisite official wording and secrecy designations.

As soon as he'd compiled a list he thought would embody both believability and shock, Dash cornered LeBeau at Exercise Hour and handed him an envelope with notes scratched on both sides. They listed fake documents Dash wanted to create and disseminate as soon as he could build the device to get them onto the Web.

"I'm not looking for fun," Dash told LeBeau. "I'm looking for stuff that'll create a storm inside The Boss's head and hopefully inside the entire leadership."

LeBeau was so giddy he wanted to give the project a code name to rally the Underground — "like the Normandy invasion, right?"

"Okay," Dash told him, "we'll tweak Eisenhower and call it Operation Overload. I mean we're overloading The Boss's brain with so much anger he'll explode."

LeBeau laughed. "I can see Fourth of July fireworks in whatever part of his little brain that makes emotions."

"The cerebrum," said Dash.

"Yeah. Whatever. Let's call it Operation Overload."

LeBeau lined up DLs willing to lift components from the salvage plant, and Dash recruited Sue Romano, the architect and designer, to create final documents from Eleanor's sketches. It took the team a couple of weeks to case the Resource Recovery Center and map out pathways to evade the security cameras. Dash used the time to draft a parts list. When components landed, he worked at night under his bedcovers with a small flashlight provided by Caleb Jones, who also smuggled in a small battery. Every few days, Dash would slip into the library to consult *Popular Mechanics.*

The work was painstaking and tedious in part because Dash was also working by day as a scavenger at the salvage plant and tussling weekly with Armstrong over the meaning of The Ten Grudgments. He would hand off each night's work to LeBeau, who placed the components inside the massive *Yale Shakespeare* compendium that Polly had delivered. LeBeau hollowed the book out from "*The Two Gentlemen of Verona*" to "*A Winter's Tale,*" dropped finished components inside, and kept it right out in the open on his night table. When he needed another book, he carved out the inside of a gold-adorned New Testament Bible, from *Matthew 28* to *Revelation 1*, and kept it in the night table drawer like a motel Gideon.

Dash had to husband the power of Caleb's battery, but it only took three tests of the completed device to get it to work. The final step was carried out in a darkened men's room at 3 a.m. Dash sat on a commode with his do-it-yourself masterpiece in his lap and wept tears of relief when he succeeded in connecting wirelessly to the Sanctuary router, and thence to the Web. The device was the size of a paperback copy of the novel *1984*, once a classic and now just another banned book.

Despite the bleak ending, Dash and LeBeau gave their jerry-rigged communications device a code name: "Orwell."

6

The individual whom Acton Grudge trusted most wasn't his third wife or son or daughter or physician or personal trainer or Executive Chef or meth supplier or even Gilbert Billups III, the questionably ordained pastor whom he called "my direct connection to God." The Boss's most trusted aide was Hector Saletan, his full-time fixer and permanent Chief Cleansing Officer. A former Metro cop who had served on The Boss's bodyguard detail, Saletan was a bulldog when it came to carrying out his patron's wishes. He understood that the absolute highest priority for The Boss was finding his critics and neutralizing them. He'd been spearheading The Great Cleansing and acting as the premier hatchet man for The Boss for nearly two decades.

As Chief Cleansing Officer, Saletan had access to all the investigative power of the Boss Bureau of Investigation. He could get warrants from the Chief Law and Order Officer to conduct wiretaps and home searches and banking inquiries. He could tap the substantial manpower and weaponry controlled by the Chief Military Officer. He could read tax returns handed over by the Chief Treasury Officer. He could even requisition tracts of land from the Chief Agriculture Officer to build new Sanctuaries.

He was so close to The Boss that if Saletan asked any member of The Board to get on his or her knees and sing Dixie, they'd ask: in what key?

Saletan was born into a family of Catholic cops. His grandfather was one of the early Metro Enforcers, and his father was an Enforcer as well. Two of his five brothers were Enforcers. One reported to The Boss's Interior Enforcement Agency and the other to the BBI Support Squad. At the dinner table growing up, most of what they heard included gritty stories of confrontations with suspected lawbreakers of one sort or another. Hector was in and out of street gangs as a teenager, which at times put him in direct conflict with his father, who would wrestle him to the basement and shove him against the cinderblock wall to teach him a lesson. Once, his dad handcuffed him to a gas pipe and kicked him so hard the boy saw blood in his urine. At eighteen, Hector took a job as a bouncer, and at twenty his dad fudged the boy's arrest record so he could work as a Metro Enforcer himself.

Hector loved the uniform, but he gave it up when the Mayor, who happened to be an ardent Boss Lover, hired him off the street squad to be part of the city's Metropolitan Protective Service, a unit of plainclothes bodyguards. The Mayor had a habit of assigning occasional non-germane tasks to his bodyguards, like picking up his dry cleaning or "having a frank discussion" with a city contractor trying to raise prices. The "frank discussions" became Hector's specialty. He was extremely effective at achieving the desired outcome.

So it was a no-brainer when The Boss asked his friend the Mayor to recommend a few people with smarts and muscle to come down to the capital and join the Federal Protective Service. Hector was thrilled and took to the task like a ravenous dog to a fresh bone. The Boss treated him like a son and became, in Hector's mind, the father he should have had. The bond of loyalty was rock solid. It wasn't long after Hector took over the regional Cleansing Squad when The Boss asked him to run the national squad. Hector became Chief Cleansing Officer and sat on the regime's Board. Only in America.

Hector was built like an inverted triangle: massive shoulders and torso, a trim waist that he maintained with daily workouts, unusually short legs, and tiny feet. He almost never combed his hair, and it sometimes made him look like a madman. There wasn't a man or woman in The Boss's inner circle who considered Saletan's word to be anything but a hundred percent gold bullion. If he got in someone's face and threatened to rip off their testicles, you knew he meant it. Nobody even thought about crossing him.

Of course, Saletan never questioned The Boss, and his parting words when the two met were always: "You got it, Boss. When do you need it?"

Whenever he was summoned by The Boss, Saletan immediately stopped what he was doing and got on an encrypted phone line. In the case of in-person meetings, he raced into The Boss's office, the Do It Room, as soon as was humanly possible and always with a gesture of humility. It took him eight minutes and fifteen seconds to get from his capital townhouse to the door of the Do It Room, give or take thirty seconds.

The Board's meeting day was Wednesday, so Saletan was in town when The Boss surprised him with a phone call at 6 a.m.

"Some bad shit is happening, Saletan."

"Yeah, Boss? We'll straighten it out."

"Come see me."

"Eight minutes."

"Make it five."

The Boss was pacing and mumbling to himself when Saletan breezed past Rosie, The Boss's secretary, and the two uniformed sentries at the main entrance to the Do It Room. It was barely light outside and the curtains were drawn, as always. The Boss kept the lights dimmed and the curtains drawn so that little of the Do It Room's ceremonial grandeur captured the attention of visitors and staff. The Boss loved his busts of Stonewall Jackson and Vince Lombardi but hated being upstaged by them. The one person, dead or alive, who commanded attention in the Do It Room was Acton Grudge.

"I've been up all fucking night, Heck," The Boss complained, rubbing the folds of his neck. "Sit down," he commanded.

"Why didn't you call me earlier?" Saletan inquired.

"Ah, fuck it."

Saletan sat and The Boss settled into a wing chair, exhaling deeply as his rear hit the cushion, as if the burdens of leadership in the mega-church of Bossism were overwhelming him.

"Okay. What gives?"

"Here's the deal, Heck. Somebody's out to fuck me over."

"Well, of course they are, Boss. You mean more than usual?"

"Hell, yes, I mean more than usual."

"Okay."

"Did you know I've got some eggheads working for me? I mean smart asses who are trying to come across as regular people."

"Smart asses?"

"Yeah, I mean educated people, super educated, more educated than they let on."

"Ah, that's bad..."

"Fuck, yeah, it's bad! And they're lying about their credentials. I mean I don't want anybody telling me what to do who thinks they're smarter than me."

"Plus, it looks real bad."

"Fuck yeah, it looks bad. I'm a man of the people, right? Everyday guy. No discussions of grandeur."

"Delusions of grandeur."

"What'd I say?"

"Discussions of grandeur."

"And that's what I fuckin' meant! Jesus..."

"Sorry Boss. Absolutely. Discussions of grandeur. But, whaddaya mean they're lying about it?"

"I mean they're not telling the truth, for fuck's sake. About how many advanced degrees they have! Passing themselves off as average Joes with just street-smarts. If this gets out...if it gets out that I'm surrounded by PhDs and people with fucking educations, like Master's Degrees, and goddamn *summa cum laude*, I'm fucked, ya know?"

"I know, Boss. I know. Who's got these egghead degrees and how'd you find out?"

"A bunch of 'em, apparently."

"Yeah?"

"Get this. Costa, the Deputy Chief Economy Officer. Costa happened to be in here last night for a meeting on the Bosseconomy. So I asked him, and he confessed that he'd hidden the fact that he has a fucking PhD in economics!"

"Costa?"

"Yeah! Asshole. I fired him on the spot. I never liked the way he talked to me. I suspected him. But I never thought to ask where he went to school when we sent his name over for confirmation."

"Never mattered, did it."

"Who gives a fuck what college?"

"Right," said Saletan. "But if they're hiding elitist credentials, then they might be planning elitist programs, right?"

"That's the point, Heck! And they might do something so fancy no one but them understands it! I can't have that."

"No way."

"Some deputy gets a bright idea and convinces the Chief Officer, ya know? I didn't pick the Chiefs to get shit done. I picked them to take orders. I don't need some deputy with a secret PhD telling a Chief to put a plan in place. Jesus."

"No way."

"I had Rosie pull out the resume Costa gave us two years ago, and I asked him: 'Is this right?' And he confessed it wasn't, the fucker."

"Tell me how you found out about this, Boss."

"It's all over the Dark Web. Somebody put some crap on the Web."

"But where'd they get it?"

"Somebody leaked a document. A fucking document."

"Can I see it?"

"Yeah."

The Boss rose gingerly from his chair. He was showing his age. His hair was dyed but lines of gray were creeping in. He was wearing bedroom slippers instead of his usual oxfords with lifts. Unlike his public performance persona, where he stood as straight as he could, The Boss was bent and weary-looking. He shuffled to his desk to retrieve a piece of paper.

"Here."

Saletan, who despised the reading glasses his doctor had prescribed, pressed his nose into the paper and scanned.

"What the fuck."

"See what I mean, Heck?"

"What the fuck."

"See what I fucking mean?"

The paper was a spreadsheet labeled "Office of Personnel: Executive Credentials" at the top. It had the regime's seal in the upper right corner. And it was stamped: "Ultra Secret." Neither The Boss nor Saletan had ever seen it. The rows listed government agencies and departments and the column headings, from left to right, listed types of university degrees: Doctorate, Master's, Bachelor's, Law Degree, Doctor of Jurisprudence, Doctor of Christology, Medical Degree, No Higher Ed. There were no names, just numbers in each cell. In the Economy row, the number of Doctorate degrees was eleven and master's degrees twenty-seven.

"Jesus," Saletan said.

"You see that? Eleven Doctorate degrees in Economy?"

"Nobody needs that."

"We gotta watch the Dark Web, Heck. I don't need this shit bubbling up where people can see it. And we gotta plug the fucking leak. Who the hell leaked that spreadsheet? I need to know who."

"I'll put some people on it. We'll find the leaker. We'll trace it back. We'll see whose fingerprints are on it."

"And chop their fucking hands off."

"We'll find 'em, Boss."

"If it turns out to be the Chinese again, you let me know, okay?"

"Who else knows about this, Boss? We'll deny it, right? We'll disavow the document. It's fake, right? Nobody will care if Costa's gone. He's a big fat nobody."

"Exactly. As far as you and I are concerned, and anyone else, the spreadsheet is fake, Heck. We deny it. We'll deport Costa, make him disappear. What kind of a name is that, anyway? Just get back to me when you know something."

"You got it, Boss. When do you need it?"

"Yesterday, Heck. I need it yesterday."

It wasn't the only time The Boss had to summon Saletan in the next three weeks. More embarrassing leaked documents landed on the Dark Web. Saletan thought his team might be closing in on the perpetrators when The Boss went full nutzoid one morning. He phoned Hector Saletan in a burning rage.

"Heck, godammit. Get the fuck over here!"

Shit, Saletan thought, The Boss is gonna have a coronary.

"What's up, Boss?"

"They're tryin' to castrate me, godammit! Just get over here."

As he entered the Do It Room, panting, Saletan asked, "What's this about castration, Boss?"

"Jesus Fucking Christ, Heck. They've gone too far this time. Bastards. Everyone knows Venus and I've been trying to have another son for years, right? Boss Junior is a dullard and a fuck-up. I need another boy. That's all I'm asking for. Now, they've started a rumor that I can't get it up anymore and need shots to, you know, to..."

"Well, that's obviously bullshit."

"Yeah, it's bullshit alright. They're jealous, right? That's it. But it's in a document again. A fake document."

"We deny it, right? Call it fake."

"Of course we do! Fucking Dark Web. Shit just lands and somebody puts it on social media."

"What'd the document say?"

"It's a prescription for injections with *my* name on it. It names the drugs and everything."

"Injections?"

"Why the hell are you looking at me like that, Heck? Yeah, injections. That's what I said. Injections. And they fucking hurt."

"They hurt?"

"Yeah. Jesus. I read about it, okay? Didn't believe it at first, so I read about it, okay? They fucking put a needle, you know, right in your junk so you can do the deed."

"Oh."

"And that's not all. These fuckers put other shit on the Dark Web."

"Like what?"

"They posted some kind of genetic analysis, supposedly ordered by the First Physician, Doc Phelps, the same one whose name is on the prescription. We gotta investigate that guy. Anyway, this genetic analysis shows I'm not all White but one-eighth Afroasiatic. Whatever the fuck that is. Not White, anyway. And it's already getting millions of hits!"

"Jesus."

"I look White, don't I, Heck?"

"Of course you do."

"Damn right. But wait, wait, wait. They faked some sort of reimbursement invoices from the event company that puts on my Freedom Assemblies. And you know what they show? Big fucking Participation Payments to people hauled in off the street to fill seats at my rallies. Thousands of them. You hearing that? People at *my* rallies who were holding up signs like 'Shut-up-ism For All' were *paid* to be there. I had no idea, Heck! I thought they were all in love with me. What the fuck? Did you know that, Heck?"

"Of course I didn't, Boss. That really sucks."

Saletan had never seen a hint of a crack in his relationship with The Boss, but now he could see the man was hurting and his trust was beginning to fray.

"And one more," The Boss sighed.

"Another one?"

"Yeah, these sons of bitches have been hard at work, Heck. They dropped some supposedly secret BBI report that says the headquarters of the League of Christian Voters might be running — listen to this — a sex-trafficking operation. Can you believe that? And it looks real! The report looks real!"

"Oh, fuck."

"Heck, you need to find out where this shit's coming from, and fast." He pointed a crooked finger at Saletan. "The Boss Haters, right? The Underground, right? They're behind this, and I don't know why you haven't figured it out and brought these assholes in. What are you doing?"

Saletan got defensive. It was a mistake.

"Trust me, Boss. We're all over it. Doing the best we can. We'll put more resources on it. But we need evidence to make it fly in court."

"Goddamn courts. I should have subdued the courts years ago, but I'm working on it. Some of these judges are older than I am. They think they should follow the fucking Criminal Code instead of common sense. I need a few more years to weed them out. But it's gonna happen. Mark my words."

"You bet, Boss. No stone unturned. I must have a hundred wiretaps out already. I've been doing house searches. The BBI is all over it. We're putting up reward money, checking Sanctuaries, and getting employers to search company emails. We'll expand everything. The spreadsheet on credentials was totally fake, right? But they must have known about Costa. Maybe they did. It's hard to know until we bring 'em in and use some Supplemental Persuasion Methods."

"I don't care what it takes, Heck. Put a stopper in this, you hear me? The Dark Web is a cesspool. If you can't find evidence, make up the goddamned evidence."

The Boss started coughing. "Read my lips!" he wheezed. "Make up the goddamned evidence!"

"Okay, Boss. Will do. You got it. Take it easy, if you can. Stay calm. We'll handle it."

As Saletan skittered out, The Boss coughed some more and shook his head. He was still fuming. Maybe it was time to put some muscle on Hector Saletan, he thought — an incentive to nail the bastards and clean up this mess without delay or excuses.

He had the means. The Boss used financial leverage all the time to get what he wanted, but he'd never resorted to it with the man he trusted most in the world. To make certain Saletan was amply compensated for his loyal service, The Boss had structured the job of Chief Cleansing Officer so that the officeholder received a bounty for every DL sent to a Sanctuary and every brown-skinned migrant shoved over the border into Pacifica or sent back to where he or she had come from.

This was the way things were now done in the Capital. Whatever you could grab as your own was fair game. It was a mark of your power, and power was everything — the power to bend someone to your will. As soon as the average Passivist decided they either didn't understand or care about conflicts of interest and corruption in government, it was a field day for grifters. The only thing that mattered was the amount of money in one's wallet or the power to command others to open theirs and fork over dues.

The entire concept of incentive, which flourished in the private sector, had already transformed the public sector into a segment of the Bosseconomy where greed, conflicts of interest, strong-arm tactics, bribery, and extortion were commonplace and expected. The Boss didn't bother to distinguish between those among his loyalists who yearned for all things POSSible because they truly believed in Prayer, Order, Security, and Shut-up-ism, and those loyalists who pretended to believe because they knew they could cash in. In any case, all the talk about bringing private sector methods into the public sector to make it more efficient became a religion under The Boss. The man in the street bought into all of it because Bossism was measured by its pragmatism in getting to a final "deal," not the methods used to get the deal done. Only sissies believed in rules and respected the prerogatives of others.

The regime's Board consisted of all the Chief Officers, each of whom operated like a corporate CEO. Just as the Chief Cleansing Officer was paid for every person he could designate as a Deranged Lunatic, the Chief Agriculture Officer's pay was linked to crop yields, the Chief Transportation Officer was paid according to potholes patched and bridges bolstered, the Chief Diplomatic Officer by the number of treaties abrogated, the Chief Media Officer by words censored, and the Chief Espionage Officer by documents declared "Hyper Secret," "Ultra Secret," or "Never Existed."

The Chief Law and Order Officer was paid according to cases won in court, but it was a particularly tough job because The Boss hadn't yet expended much political capital bending the Judiciary to his will. Through his appointment powers, he had already named thousands of Boss-loyal judges, and he didn't want to risk a backlash by going after all the old-timers in black robes. Some of the holdovers caused trouble from time to time, but The Boss knew that problem judges eventually die, and he thought he'd outlive them all.

In return for these generous incentive pay packages, each of the regime's Chief Officers was beholden to The Boss but also to the League of Christian Voters. Every Chief Officer was expected to contribute three percent of his or her total annual compensation to the League, all tax deductible, and five percent to the Everything Is POSSible Fund, a trust for the benefit of The Boss's immediate family. At one time, these would have been called kickbacks, but under Bossism it was business as usual and nobody gave it a second thought.

The Boss loved to declare that "my government is run just like a business!" That's all he needed to say. If you worshipped Jesus and Free Enterprise, everything was good and efficient. It made The Boss's army of Passivists believe his regime was clean as a white whistle.

There was one little-known brake on exorbitant pay packages or on Chief Officers whom The Boss thought might be getting overly greedy. It was called the Central Statistics Bureau, an agency controlled exclusively by The Boss. Chief Officers didn't account for their own good deeds in service to the regime. The CSB did. All the

Deranged Lunatic cases, crop yields, court cases won, potholes patched, treaties abrogated, and words censored, etc., were enumerated by the CSB. So, if The Boss wanted to exert some muscle on one of his Chief Officers, he simply instructed the CSB to make an adjustment to the numbers, which had the effect of lowering the Officer's incentive pay. This instruction was called a Boss-Ordered Fiscal Fudge, or BOFF.

Not once had Hector Saletan been BOFFed, his bond to The Boss was so great. Yet The Boss was so furious at Saletan's seeming inability to cauterize the wounds being created by all the reverse disinformation that he considered a BOFF just for Hector. He even drafted a hand-written memo in the Do It Room. But before the memo reached the Central Statistics Bureau, Saletan's investigation seemed to hit pay dirt. He requested an emergency meeting to brief The Boss.

"We think we got something, Boss," Saletan opened in the dimness of the Do It Room.

"The Underground?"

"Probably. I've suspected them from the start."

"Wait. Don't tell me. Because they're the only ones clever enough to produce fake documents that can pass for real. The only ones with the balls to keep putting this stuff out in the face of almost certain detection and prosecution. The only ones smart enough to use the Dark Web to launder the fucking documents and get them onto social media. Do I have it right, Heck?"

The Boss was wheezing he was so angry.

"Yes. All of that, Boss. Are you okay?"

The Boss coughed a deep cough. "I'd be okay if I knew what the fuck was taking you so long."

"Well, the BBI has questioned hundreds of Sanctuary staff and run lie-detector tests. The problem is that Halcitol has properties that help mask the blood pressure, respiration, and heart rate changes that make polygraphs so effective."

"When you're happy, you're happy." He coughed again.

"Exactly, and you can lie to your heart's content without much detectable anxiety."

"But you're closing in, right? Fuckin' tell me you're closing in."

"Yeah, we are. We interviewed staff members at all thirty-seven Sanctuaries, and the BBI discovered some employees whose answers smelled funny. I ordered polygraph tests on all of them."

"Get to the fucking point, Heck!"

"Okay. We think we hit the jackpot at Sanctuary Thirteen. One employee failed the polygraph test miserably."

"And?"

"I've got the best BBI interrogator on it, Roger Thorn. He's meeting this guy Monday morning."

"About fucking time!" The Boss coughed. "This isn't prank stuff anymore, Heck. This shit is cutting to the bone, you hear?"

"I hear ya, Boss. I hear ya."

Saletan pasted a big smile on his face, but his neck, armpits, and palms were moist as he sped out of the Do It Room, knowing that, for the first time, he was under the uncomfortably hot klieg lights of Acton Grudge's anxious expectations.

7

"Well, Mr. Caleb Jones. I've been eager to meet you," said the BBI's top Convincer, Special Agent Roger Thorn, as he paced back and forth in a crisp blue suit and regulation white shirt inside Room 207, the Behavioral Health office at Sanctuary Thirteen. Thorn looked like a guy in the Marine reserves who worked out twice a day, because that is who he was. Thorn was purposeful and at times jovial, but Caleb had a strong feeling this would not go well. Saletan, who had ordered the use of Supplemental Persuasion Methods and given Thorn forty-eight hours to scour all of the regime's databases, sat nervously behind the two-way mirror, viewing the performance with the fascination of a kid watching *Perry Mason* reruns to pick up interrogation tips.

"My colleagues tell me you've worked here at Thirteen for four years and have a close-to-spotless record, Caleb," Thorn opened. "But something's happened that's cast a big shadow over everything you've achieved. And that's the polygraph test. It was pure shit, Caleb. I don't think I've ever seen a worse result. I bet you think it's the goddamn machine. But there's another possibility, isn't there, Caleb. Maybe you're hiding something. Maybe you're lying to protect someone. Maybe you're lying your ass off. It's my job to find out, and here's the naked truth, Caleb. I *always* find out. I always have and I always will. You're not going to be any different. There's not gonna be any stroke of luck here. When I'm done with you, you'll be begging me to confess. That's a promise, Caleb, from me to you."

"I ain't done nothin' wrong," Caleb said dismissively, turning his head away from Thorn to stare at the pale green wall.

Thorn stopped pacing and placed both hands gently on the table in front of Caleb. He leaned in until his nose was nearly touching Caleb's, and shouted: "You don't speak til I tell you to speak, Caleb! Understand?"

Caleb pushed himself back with a start, and his chair nearly toppled. His sense of dread sharpened, and his left eyelid began to twitch.

"Shut-up-ism is a good thing, Caleb, when I'm talking. You speak when I ask you to speak. Now let's get a few things straight." Thorn's eyes narrowed. "Number One. Boss Haters are putting out documents about The Boss, every one of them a lie, and we're gonna find out right here, today, who those Haters are. Number Two. You owe your job to The Boss and nobody else. If he says he doesn't think you're doing a good enough job, your ass is fired. Number Three. The Boss knows where you live. He knows your wife Agnes. He knows Agnes is in treatment for Parkinson's. He knows your daughter Simone and where she lives. He knows Simone is married to Jayden, who works at the hardware store. He knows Simone is pregnant, due in six weeks. And he knows your granddaughter Jillian and what school Jillian attends."

Caleb looked down and mouthed the words, "You fuckers." Thorn wasn't done.

"The Boss knows what's in your tax return. He knows what prescriptions you and Agnes take. He knows your checking account right now has eighteen-hundred bitdollars in it. He even knows your car payment on that shitty hybrid you drive. Two-thirty-eight a month. Number Four. The Boss and I can make life miserable for you, for Agnes, for Simone, for Jayden, even for little Jillian. All I have to do is pick up the phone and call him. Take me about two minutes. And finally, Number Five. You get to choose, Caleb. You can keep up this 'I ain't done nothin' wrong' bullshit, which will ensure that I make that call to The Boss, or you can tell us what you know about these fake documents and who's behind them and testify against the perpetrators in court. And for cooperating, we decide not to charge you with treason or seditious conspiracy and let you off with a suspended sentence, even though you'll never work again at a Sanctuary. You'll qualify for a year's worth of free Halcitol, too. I can make that happen. So, it's your choice, Caleb. I'm gonna be real generous and give you fifteen minutes to decide. You got two options. One, it gets real ugly for you and your family — I mean real ugly, Caleb — or two, you walk out with a suspended sentence, all the Halcitol you want, and a job somewhere else. Nothing in between. No amendments or footnotes or caveats. No what-ifs. Black or white. Up or down. Right or left. I'm walking back in here in fifteen minutes to take your answer, Caleb. You better have one. Look at the clock on the wall. Fifteen minutes."

When Thorn walked into the room behind the two-way mirror, Saletan pulled him into a corner and whispered: "What odds do you give this?"

"If he knows something, and I think he does, he'll break," Thorn whispered back.

Saletan was in Thorn's face. "He'd better break, or I'll have your fucking job, Thorn. You understand?"

Thorn didn't flinch. "He'll break. I can tell. Getting into all of the personal family business usually does the trick."

They sat down and watched Caleb through the mirror. He was already sobbing and had his hands clasped behind his neck, rubbing as if he were massaging an insistent point of severe pain.

Ten minutes later, when Caleb gave up the names Clary LeBeau and Dashiel Askin to Agent Thorn, he did so solemnly, then wept some more. With the exception of two facts, he managed to avoid coughing up anything about the jerry-rigged phone. First, he acknowledged providing the battery. Second, he recalled that LeBeau and Dash had referred to the device as "Orwell," a name that meant nothing to Caleb or Thorn until the agent conducted some research and learned this Orwell fella had been a journalist. Over and over again, Caleb told Thorn he had no idea how the documents had gotten onto the Dark Web or that the phone and the documents were connected. He only knew that LeBeau and Dash were the ones spearheading the Royal Fucking. He stuck to that story.

What choice did Caleb have? There wasn't a soul alive who thought The Boss was bluffing when he threatened someone, directly or through the BBI. It was part of the Bossism creed, one of the uglier iterations of the human form: to get your way, hurt some people in public to spread fear.

As soon as Thorn closed his notebook, Caleb asked for his first shot of Halcitol. BBI agents escorted him to the local jail and charged him with treason, seditious conspiracy, and lying to an agent of the BBI just to keep him behind bars. Then, prosecutors started drafting an immunity agreement that would allow him to escape prosecution in return for his testimony against Dash and LeBeau.

Caleb was a broken man, and when Agnes came to visit him in jail, he cried and cried. There were so many tears, he could barely explain himself to her. She'd known nothing about his escapades at Thirteen as a conduit for the Underground masquerading as a loyal Boss Lover. When she learned what he'd been doing, she didn't scream or kick him. Instead, she told him how proud she was, which shocked Caleb.

"I thought you'd kill me, Agnes."

"I hate those people," Agnes said. "Racist hoodlums."

"Why didn't you say nuthin'?"

"We talked about it, baby. You knew I hated everything about Bossism."

"But I thought you wanted me to take that job at the Sanctuary."

"I did. We were hurtin'. I knew you didn't like it. What choice did we have after the farm went under? Sometimes, you gotta do what you gotta do."

"So, why're you proud of me? Now, I'm out of a job."

"I'm proud you were doin' things against The Boss, that's all."

"But I squealed on the DLs, Agnes. I spilled my guts."

"Nothin' we can do about it now. I'm sorry you had to give up your friends, Caleb. Just tell me why. Why'd you tell the BBI the truth? Was it to protect us?"

"'Course it was, Agnes. They threatened me something awful. They threatened you, they threatened Simone and Jayden, and they even threatened Jillian. And they'd do it, too. Those are The Boss's men. They don't mess around."

"I know, baby. I told you those are bad men. Really bad men. I mean, I know you were trying to protect us, but next time they threaten you, I'm giving my permission so you can tell 'em to just fuck off."

"It's easy to say but it's a lot harder to do," Caleb said grimly.

"I know, baby. I know."

For the next three days, the all-male BBI investigative team questioned Dash and LeBeau separately and scoured Thirteen for evidence, using gadgets that emitted sonar-like waves to see into walls and tearing through everyone's personal belongings. They found the hollowed-out Shakespeare and the Bible. Both were empty. All the other DLs denied having anything to do with the scheme. That was the plan if someone got caught.

The two target perpetrators fingered by Caleb Jones insisted they were innocent, too, and demanded to see lawyers. Thorn laughed at them both.

"A lawyer? That quaint little bit about having access to counsel when you're arrested went out the window thirty years ago," he told Dash. "You're gonna talk, and you don't need anyone holding your hand."

When the agents found Orwell in the ceiling of the men's room on the same hall as the room where the two men slept, they discovered fingerprints. Inside the device's memory was one other document Dash had teed up to go onto the Dark Web the day Caleb cracked. It purported to show a memo in which The Boss quietly ordered all the crosses, Bibles, and likenesses of Jesus Christ removed from his private living quarters inside Hollywood House.

While Thorn questioned Dash, Special BBI Agent Johnny Bell took on LeBeau.

"We found the phone you made in the ceiling of the men's room, and your fingerprints are all over it, LeBeau," Bell explained, unwrapping a black felt cloth that contained a plastic bag with the device inside. "So there's no point anymore in denying your role."

"Well, good for you boys," LeBeau said. "Only took you, what, two days? You had fifteen agents turning this place upside down. Doesn't prove shit, though. What makes you think I made it? How do you know I didn't pick up that piece of plastic cover as part of my job in the Resource Recovery Center? Ever think of that, Agent Bell? Those components don't exist in the salvage plant as virgins, you know, without ever being touched."

"And you think a jury is going to believe that bullshit?"

"Didn't say that. Boss Juries will believe anything they're spoon-fed. So you can make up all the evidence you want. But the truth is, I didn't have anything to do with the stuff The Boss is pissing about."

"That's not what Dash Askin is telling us."

"Sure."

"Thorn just talked to him and he gave a full confession, implicating you. Said you're the one who stole the components, built the phone, created the documents, and uploaded them to the Web. You, LeBeau. Nobody else. He says he just found a hiding place for the parts."

"False, and you know it."

"Think about it, LeBeau. He's already agreed to testify against you in return for a guilty plea to desecrating a Bible. The one he hollowed out for you to store all your components."

"False."

"Suit yourself, LeBeau. I'm a generous guy, so I'll give you four hours to think about it. Either I come back at 3 p.m. and take your confession or you get sent up for treason, sedition, and seven counts of slander after a trial in which Caleb Jones and Dashiel Askin testify against you. You'll be in prison for the rest of your life. Your choice, LeBeau. See you at 3. The guard will bring you some water."

At 2:55 p.m., LeBeau shouted through the locked door that he had written a confession and wanted to speak to Agent Bell. When Bell walked in, LeBeau handed him two pieces of paper.

"Read it. It's my confession."

"Alright, LeBeau. I see you've come to your senses."

"I never left my senses."

Bell sat down and looked first at the end of the handwritten confession. It was dated and bore LeBeau's signature. This pleased Bell. Then he began to read from the beginning.

I, Clary LeBeau, being of sound mind and body, hereby state: I am a DL at Sanctuary Thirteen. I don't trust liars, con men, bullies, or idiots posing as wise elders. I refuse to accept police-state tactics, invasions of privacy, propaganda aimed at thought control, or fake Christianity.

Bell glared at LeBeau then turned back to the end of the material. Above his signature, LeBeau had written:

I confess that I'd rather rot in prison than kiss the ass of The Boss or any of his BBI henchmen.

Bell sat shaking his head slowly, side to side, like a parent watching his teenage son fail the driving test. He crumpled up the two pages and flipped them back at LeBeau, who was grinning broadly, enjoying every minute. The wadded-up paper hit him in the shoulder and fell to the floor. LeBeau handed Bell his pencil.

Thorn's interrogation of Dash took place in Armstrong's office, with two armed Monitors posted outside and four BBI agents watching from behind the two-way mirror. Thorn walked up to Dash with the same felt cloth containing the phone the agents had found. He placed it on the desk in front of Dash and unfolded the cloth.

"Recognize this, Askin?"

"Your tape recorder? Looks kind of old."

"It's the phone device you made from parts stolen from the Resource Recovery Center."

"Looks like a good job by someone."

"Someone? That's not what LeBeau told us. He said you stole the parts, built the phone, connected it to the Web, and uploaded the documents."

"Nobody could have built a phone from scrap parts. That's impossible."

"We tested it, Askin. Works pretty well, well enough to upload files to the Web. You did a good job."

"Somebody must have, but it wasn't me."

In his youth, Dash had never thought of himself as a risk-taker. It was only when he saw the risks his parents took that he began to consider the reward side of the equation. He came to believe that recklessness could only be measured against the potential gains of an act. Were his parents reckless? There might be rewards beyond one's self, but the only sure reward was measured as self-worth, and Dash knew that self-worth was closely aligned with conscience. His parents had taught him that much. Even so, deep inside, Dash was in turmoil. This could be the end of the road, he thought.

Thorn played his ace. "What if I told you we found your fingerprints on the device."

"So?"

"Pretty damning evidence. A phone that can connect to the Web has your fingerprints all over it, plus a fake document in the memory."

"All the fingerprints prove is that I worked in the Resource Recovery Center and touched parts in the course of my job. That's what I'm supposed to do. I'd say whoever built that phone, if it's real, is a genius. Do I look like a genius to you? And whoever sent those documents to the Web has balls. That's for sure. I'm too chickenshit to do something like that."

"LeBeau is gonna testify against you, Askin. He's agreed to do that in return for pleading guilty to desecrating a Bible. That's where you stored the parts, didn't you."

"The only things in that Bible are a few nice poems and a ton of hypocrisy."

"It's not just LeBeau. Caleb Jones is gonna testify against you, too."

"I'm sure you've told them what to say."

"You are truly Deranged, Askin. You'll be sent up for treason, sedition, and seven counts of slander and spend the rest of your life in prison."

"I'll take my chances in court with a good lawyer."

"What makes you think any lawyer will take your case? It's a sinkhole."

Dash was too savvy to believe that LeBeau would turn on him. He wanted to be an example to the Underground, not a guy trying to save himself or buy a reduced sentence. He had no remorse. Dash considered his Royal Fucking — building the phone and pumping out fake documents — to have been the most beautiful thing he'd ever done outside of creating Lily and sabotaging software at CompuLink.

Thorn got right into Dash's face the way he'd gotten into Caleb's.

"Askin, you don't fool me one bit. We know you built that device and we know you used it to post slanderous documents on the Web. The jurors are gonna see your fingerprints. We're gonna keep investigating inside Thirteen to find out who your accomplices were. We know about one, LeBeau. There were others, weren't there. Someone's gonna spill. Trust me. Someone's gonna tell us how you got the parts. Someone's gonna tell us who helped you build that phone. Someone's gonna tell us who created those documents and where they're hidden."

Dash loved sparring with Thorn, loved goading the BBI man.

"Hell, if I had done this job, I'd have thrown the documents away after I uploaded the images. Maybe they're in the dumpster outside right now. Maybe you should have your boys dive in there and look."

"Maybe you should shut up."

"Can you just tell me, Agent Thorn, why you tolerate The Boss? You're a lot smarter than he is. I bet you're a genuine Christian, too, not a fake one like Acton Grudge. Maybe you go to church on Sunday. I bet you teach your kids decent values."

"Shut up, Askin. Shut your mouth."

Dash's itch was as strong as ever. "I bet you've even heard of Lincoln and Jefferson and Roosevelt and Reagan. People to emulate."

Thorn grabbed Dash's shirt and nearly lifted him out of his chair.

"Shut your mouth, punk, or I'll shut it for you."

He pushed Dash back down in disgust. A studied calmness washed across Dash's face as he smoothed out his shirt from the manhandling.

"Go ahead, Thorn. Bust my mouth. Leave me bloody in here. But first, just tell me why in the world you take orders from a stupid, vulgar man like The Boss. You're better than that. I know you are."

Thorn cocked his head and looked at Dash from the side. He started nodding his head slowly, as if a brilliant thought had just come to him.

"We're done here, Askin. If you want to tell me the truth, call for the guard. Otherwise, clear your calendar. You're going to prison for a long, long time."

As Thorn walked to the door, Dash called: "Just look in the mirror one day and tell me what you see!"

8

The defense attorney Polly hired for Dash and LeBeau was an eighty-two-year-old ex-Deranged Lunatic from the rural Carolinas whose law office was a folding table inside a storefront next to a Sunoco station flying the Boss Nation flag. She knew his story and never considered anyone else. William "Wild Bill" Abrams was an anomaly. He was the first and only DL to have appealed his Derangement Hearing conviction and won — not his freedom but simply the right to serve as his own attorney during his re-hearing and appeal.

Wild Bill was a natural-born orator with a steel-trap mind and made verbal mincemeat of anyone who stood in his way. Ultimately, the Supreme Court upheld his sentence of five years in Sanctuary One, but along the way the Bossist majority on the Court was reluctant to declare that he had no right to counsel and, further, no right to serve as his own attorney. By a slim majority, the Justices upheld The Boss's edict that no defense attorneys could be present at Derangement Hearings but then created a new category of Derangement just for Wild Bill so that he could be the exception.

The Court reasoned that Wild Bill's intellect and powers of persuasion warranted creation of a unique strain of the social disease. They called it Self-Derangement. According to the court, a Self-Deranged Lunatic wasn't like every other plain-vanilla DL, who had obviously fallen ill in cult-like obedience to the outmoded idea of liberal democracy. The court said a Self-Deranged Lunatic possessed unique intellectual defenses against following the herd and was just sane enough to mount his or her own defense but not so sane that walking the streets could be deemed risk-free for society at large.

At the time, the reigning theory among leading jurisprudologists was that the Court couldn't get enough of Wild Bill's theater, complete with rhetorical flourishes and white untrimmed eyebrows that flew up and down with each new thought. The Justices couldn't resist encouraging more of it for their own amusement in an otherwise tedious life on the rubber-stamp bench.

Naturally, The Boss was furious when the Court issued its ruling handing Wild Bill an exemption, and he took his revenge. The Boss arranged for Hector Saletan to leak documents to BTV revealing that Chief Justice Maxwell Frank, author of the Court's majority opinion on Wild Bill, had been born Jewish, converted to Christianity, and married a closet Latina who entered the country illegally. BTV anchors went on a rampage, demanding that Bettina Frank release her birth certificate. When the Chief Justice abruptly filed for divorce, claiming Bettina had shacked up with a wrangler while the couple was on an all-expenses-paid holiday at a dude ranch near Phoenix, he won an element of sympathy, and the bonfire of accusations fizzled and died. Chief Justice Frank survived with his black robe unsullied. Not so his ex-wife. As Chief Cleansing Officer, Hector Saletan went after Bettina, and she ended up on a plane to Bolivia in an orange jumpsuit and zip-tie handcuffs, her every move broadcast on BTV.

Polly had never met LeBeau, but when she visited Dash in jail shortly after he was charged, he urged her to find someone willing to defend both of them. Dash evidently thought Wild Bill was dead and came up with a few other names. But Polly, recalling the Maxwell Frank hullabaloo from her youth, found Wild Bill, alive and feisty as ever. He was wearing his signature white ponytail when she sat down at his card table, and he didn't hesitate for a second when she asked him if he'd be willing to defend two fellow DLs, Dashiel Askin and Clary LeBeau.

"I'm your man, alright."

"And what would your fee be?" Polly asked.

"Shit. I don't know. Maybe we do this: nothing at all if we lose, and a good Cuban cigar if we win."

"Well, we're not made of money, so that would be very much appreciated. I'd be really thrilled if we can get to the cigar, but aren't Cuban goods banned in the U.S.?"

"I have a supplier down in Miami. How about a round-trip flight?"

"Sounds very reasonable."

Wild Bill and Polly sat together during multiple visits devising a strategy that had at least a chance of yielding an acquittal. The young and polished prosecutor in the case, George Remington Huff, had charged Dash and LeBeau with seven counts of slandering The Boss (one for each attempted Royal Fucking), one count of seditious conspiracy, and one count of conspiracy to commit treason. The penalty for each count of slander was five years.

"For starters, Miss Polly, I believe we could probably convince whichever trial judge is assigned to have them serve concurrent terms instead of consecutive ones," Wild Bill told her at one of their sessions.

"That's not exactly heartening."

"I got a lot more angles, though. I've been thinking. You always want to offer the jury an alternative to the story the prosecutor's tellin', know what I mean? It's all about the story, the narrative — what feels right."

"And what story do you have in mind?"

"It's a 'what if' until I can convince some people to testify, but what if we present these so-called Royal Fuckings as jokes, cartoons, poking fun, harmless gags? What if your husband and his sidekick weren't trying to defame The Boss at all, poor guy?"

"You mean a 'just kidding' defense?"

"Yes, ma'am. Good for you. The 'just kidding' defense. Now, that's what we could do with slander, but I need to say that sedition and treason are something else altogether. I suspect the evidence is unambiguous on those. We know Dash and LeBeau conspired. The only two sets of fingerprints found on that communication device were theirs. Even if they weren't, the prosecutor will put someone on the stand to say they were. And those boys really shoulda thought twice about giving it that Orwell name. Orwell was as anti-tyranny as they come, and Lord forgive us, he was also a journalist. The jury's not gonna like it. Even so, I do believe that if we can get the 'just kidding' defense to work, maybe — just maybe — we can convince them to drop the sedition and treason charges."

"Tell me the truth, Mr. Abrams. How realistic is that?"

"Franky, Miss Polly, it's a monumental long shot," Wild Bill told her, his eyebrows fluttering, "and one with serious consequences if it goes down in flames."

"What are the consequences exactly?" Polly asked. "I think I ought to know."

"For starters, sedition carries a life sentence, and the penalty for treason is, well, it's not good."

"Death?"

"By firing squad."

Polly sat back in her folding chair and sighed, "Oh, Dash." Wild Bill didn't miss a beat.

"Here's what we're gonna do, Miss Polly," he told her, whispering as if he thought the BBI might be listening. "We're gonna convince the best and most popular comedians in the business to come in and testify. Comics you see on BTV all the time. We're gonna find the ones willing to defend the right to tell a fuckin' joke, the right to create satire. They'll testify under oath about what makes a shtick funny and what makes one hateful and malicious. Don't you worry. Humor was their only way of surviving the horror of life as a DL, right? They were suffering and retreated into humor, right? Two fun-loving partners at Sanctuary Thirteen. Abbott and Costello, Burns and Allen, Lucy and Ricky, Dash and LeBeau. Got it, Miss Polly?"

Polly smiled wanly. "I've heard of Abbott and Costello."

"Never mind. We're gonna put the right to satire on trial, dammit," Wild Bill declared.

Polly's gut instinct told her he was creatively building a reason to be hopeful but not really constructing a serious legal defense against slander, sedition, and treason.

"Mr. Abrams, I worry that any halfway intelligent juror will see that Dash was expressing hatred and malice when he put those documents onto the Dark Web. Everything about them suggests that the aim was to erode support for The Boss and ridicule Bossism. Am I right?"

"I can't deny it, Miss Polly, but I have to build an alternative theory, you see? Give the jury something to chew on. Plant a little doubt."

Polly left that day as depressed as she had ever felt. But when she replayed her conversation with Wild Bill to Dash during a prison visit, he was ecstatic.

"You know, the Russian dissidents made a mockery of the regime right out in the open. We'll do the same thing Navalny did. We've come this far. There's no reason to hold back."

Polly wondered if it was the Halcitol but said nothing. "Don't you remember how it ended for Navalny and the others? They died or disappeared, if I recall my history correctly."

"If I'm going down, Pol, I want to go down like they did, with my honor intact and with a flourish."

"Oh, Dash, I wish you wouldn't make light of all this. It's your life we're talking about!"

"I'm sorry, hun. But how else will I keep my sanity? They're probably going to offer me a deal: something like forty years if I plead guilty to all the charges."

"Wouldn't you take it? Should I get Abrams to offer that?"

"I'd never agree to that! I can't. Think about it, sweetheart. Because of my age, it's the same as a life sentence. I'll die in prison either way. And they get a public admission of treason? A public admission of sedition and slander? Hell, no."

"I know. I know. You could never bow down like that."

"Then let's make the very best of this. I will be a happy man, Pol, if I can keep my head high and make a caricature of tyranny and take a sense of real gratification to my grave."

Polly wiped the tears from her cheeks.

"Okay, Dash. I know," she said, forcing a smile. "We'll do this together, alright? We'll make it the greatest Royal Fucking in courtroom history. I'll just have to explain it to Lily."

"That's my girl."

Dash and LeBeau pleaded not guilty before Senior Judge Richard Fullwood, who was randomly assigned the case to the delight of Wild Bill Abrams. He told his clients it was the biggest stroke of luck they could have hoped for. The judge wanted a speedy start to the trial, but Wild Bill requested four months to prepare his case. He needed to go through witness lists, evidence, and investigative notes — the process of discovery. George Huff, the straight-arrow prosecutor, wanted to start right away.

"Your honor, the evidence in this case is as narrow as it is damning," Huff argued in a confab in the judge's chambers. "We have a jerry-rigged communications device with the fingerprints of both defendants, and we have counterfeit documents, not hundreds of them but seven. And we have a clear motive for one of the defendants. His parents were Enemies of the People, arrested and convicted of serious crimes. And we have the testimony of one of their confederates at Sanctuary Thirteen. Let's get on with it."

Huff lost that argument, mostly because he hadn't been on the prep school tennis team sixty years earlier with a kid named Billy Abrams, and the future jurist Dickie Fullwood had been. The other reason was that, in private, Wild Bill had informed his friend the judge of a novel approach he might want to take to the case: searching for evidence that any of the slander charges might be mostly or entirely true.

"I've got a damned good investigator working full-time on it," Wild Bill told Fullwood, "because truth is a defense in defamation cases. If I didn't turn over every stone, I'd be doing my clients a gross disservice that could make me vulnerable to a malpractice action."

Fullwood humored his old friend. "You're being overly dramatic, Bill. But I'll give you two months. I'm bending over backward to give your clients a fair shot. Even so, I'd say you're on a fool's errand. If you're doing this *pro bono*, you'll be burning through a lot of your own cash. And jury selection won't be very satisfying for you, either."

Wild Bill left the meeting smiling. He'd gotten nearly everything he needed.

When the trial finally got underway in the high-ceilinged courtroom on the second floor of the Old Federal Building downtown, Wild Bill looked pale and slightly bent. His ponytail flopped over his shoulder. The ancient lawyer wore Sanctuary-issued gray chinos that he'd never given up, a wrinkled blue cotton blazer over an equally wrinkled white shirt, and a black knit tie. Dash and LeBeau sat to his right in bright royal blue prison jumpsuits, with the words "Upstream Penitentiary" on the back.

As Fullwood stepped to the bench, he scanned the courtroom to make sure everything was in order. The BTV cameras were running, and he guessed an audience in the tens of millions was watching live from homes and offices all over the country, maybe the world.

Dash and LeBeau stood before the judge in handcuffs, a change in courtroom protocol that The Boss had instituted as a "law and order" upgrade along with what he called a "streamlining reform" that called for judges to pick a jury rather than letting the prosecutor and defense attorney hash out the selections.

A calm smile crossed Wild Bill's face when Fullwood banged his gavel to begin opening arguments. The attorney thought he had at least one ace up his sleeve in the form of a hot-shot comedian who'd agreed to testify for the defense. He was the only one the lawyer could convince to take the stand, but it was a big name.

"Be seated," the judge instructed the two sides. A hundred or so Bossism fanatics filled the rest of the seats. Polly and Lily sat directly behind Dash and were joined by LeBeau's older sister, Maggie, who mostly dabbed her eyes, at least when she was awake.

"Let's usher in the jury, Mr. Bailiff," Fullwood nodded.

Twelve stern-looking jurors and four equally dour alternates entered the jury box, already looking burned out for a trial that was just beginning. Wild Bill wondered if he was at a wake. It was impossible to tell, either by the jurors' listed occupations or facial expressions, whether they fell fully into the Bossism camp or only partly.

"Sheeee-it," Wild Bill muttered to himself. He turned to Dash and whispered: "Never seen a jury more humorless in my life." From that moment, Wild Bill understood that his "just kidding" defense would need to be presented with the utmost seriousness.

Fullwood went through his Blessed Be The Boss formalities, and cued the prosecutor for his opening argument. Huff slathered on praise for the jurors' civic-mindedness and patience, as well as the generosity of their families in allowing each one to honor the system of justice with their participation. It was a glorious, textbook effort to butter up the jury and cloak himself as a gracious and supremely reasonable bearer of facts.

"This is one of the simplest cases I will ever try," Huff declared. "When the state is done presenting the evidence against these two defendants, you will see with perfect clarity that they maliciously slandered The Boss with smears and lies and, by their own words and deeds, conspired in a seditious and treasonous attempt —— fortunately unsuccessful — to harm my government and yours. And they did it from the safety and comfort of one of our most advanced Sanctuaries."

Huff paced back and forth along the front rail of the jury box in a tailored charcoal wool suit, crisp white French-cuffed shirt, blue striped tie, and shiny, plain-toe leather oxfords that squeaked when he walked. He glanced at the index cards in his left hand.

"Rookie," Wild Bill thought, perhaps wishfully.

"You will hear, ladies and gentlemen," Huff continued, "the testimony of Caleb Jones, a Sanctuary employee who was working in league with the defendants. You will hear that one of the defendants had a deeply personal motive to commit these acts. You will see the counterfeit documents they produced. You will hear expert testimony that traces the digital versions of those fraudulent documents straight back to a modem within a crude communications device codenamed by *these* defendants after a discredited journalist named Orwell. And you will hear expert testimony that the only sets of fingerprints found on this so-called Orwell device were those of the defendants," — Huff pointed sneeringly at the defense table — "Dashiel Askin and Clary LeBeau."

When Fullwood introduced the defense counsel, Wild Bill rose slowly. With the solemnity of a preacher on Sunday morning, he turned to the judge and announced: "Your Honor, the defense hereby moves for a directed verdict of not guilty by reason of insanity. The very state that brings this case has already baptized these poor souls as Deranged Lunatics. They wear the scarlet letter. They cannot be held responsible for any of their alleged actions."

Expressions of surprise resounded from the courtroom seats like the bleats of sheep being herded into a tight pen. Huff leaped to his feet, shouting, "Objection!" Fullwood, looking irritated, repeatedly tapped the fingertips of both hands against one another. Dash and LeBeau smiled. Wild Bill sat back down even more slowly than he'd risen, waiting for Fullwood to react.

The judge banged his gavel four times to quiet the room.

"I am instructing the jury to ignore the defense motion," Fullwood intoned, shooting a reproachful look in Wild Bill's direction. "Mr. Huff's objection is sustained. Mr. Abrams, this court will not tolerate further frivolous motions. Your clients face serious charges, and their guilt or innocence will be determined right here in this courtroom through normal procedures. I suggest you deliver your opening argument to the jury without delay."

"Certainly, Your Honor. Thank you for indulging me." Wild Bill rose again, this time more briskly, strode to the jury box, and clasped his hands behind his slightly bent back. His voluminous eyebrows were fluttering up and down, as if giving flight to each sentence.

"Ladies and gentlemen of the jury, maybe we should all put this trivial little case behind us, pack up, and go home. I'd love that. I could get back home and take a nap, have a cold Boss Beer, and think clean thoughts. I'm sure you, too, have better things to do. According to Mr. Huff, this is all just a waste of time. Open and shut. I'm not sure why he didn't move for a directed verdict of guilty on all counts! Why even bother looking at the evidence? Let's all get out our rubber stamps, ink 'em up, and mash 'em onto the sentencing order sitting in the judge's drawer, so we can get to our couches and put our feet up in front of our beloved BTV."

"Mr. Abrams..." Fullwood interrupted.

"Getting to the point, Your Honor. Now, here's why we ought not just wash our hands of this case. Take just a minute to think about it: what if everything the defendants allegedly said about Acton Grudge, a.k.a. The Boss, was uttered *in jest?* What if these two boys were having the time of their lives inside that Sanctuary, joking around and kidding The Boss? That's right, *ribbing* him. He ought to be able to take a little ribbing, shouldn't he? Mr. Huff would have you believe that life inside a Sanctuary is as blissful as an Alpine spa in August. He talked about 'safety and comfort.' He has no idea what life is like in a Sanctuary, but I do. I've been there. And let me tell you, it's a dismal world, a world where people don't *survive* without comic relief. Believe me, folks, being sent to a Sanctuary is a heavy burden. If there's one sure antidote, though, it's humor — black humor, maybe, but humor nonetheless."

"Objection!" Huff shouted. "Defense counsel is not a psychologist or sociologist or psychoanalyst!"

"Overruled, Mr. Huff. He can present alternative theories. It's up to the jury to decide where the facts lead."

"Thank you, Your Honor," Wild Bill said as he bowed toward Fullwood. "I'll just take a minute more. Folks, what Mr. Huff is telling you is not the sole, God-given explanation for why we're sittin' here. All I'm asking is that we not rule out other perfectly reasonable explanations. That's the American way, right? Or was. The prosecution has so-called experts, and so do we. In fact, you will hear from one of this country's most highly regarded comedians and satirists — I'm sure you've seen him on BTV dozens of times. And he will testify that what my clients are accused of doing — all in the belief that The Boss could take a joke — is nothing more than playful and hysterically funny ribbing."

Wild Bill wasn't quite done. The eyebrows flapped anew.

"You have to have a mighty thin skin to think that documents inserted onto the Web by two Deranged Lunatics for fun and amusement while locked up inside a dreadful Sanctuary constitute malicious slander. I mean, really. That, my friends, is *laughable*."

George Remington Huff delivered the prosecution's case as a simple exercise in connecting the dots. He set up an easel holding poster-sized photographs of the documents and an elementary-school version of a flow chart with game-board arrows supposedly following the trail of evidence. A Department of Law and Order archivist testified that Dash's parents were subversives and had died in prison, supposedly establishing the motive of revenge. A forensic computer scientist testified that each one of the fake documents pulled from the Web had originated with the Orwell device that was found bearing the fingerprints of Dash Askin and Clary LeBeau. Wild Bill noticed that a few of the jurors looked like bobblehead dolls, rhythmically nodding their heads in an "I get it" cadence as Huff used a telescoping metal pointer to show where the arrows led in case it wasn't already painfully obvious. He also counted the number of times Huff employed the phrase "malicious lies" during the ninety-minute performance: seventeen.

Dash watched the show with growing apprehension. At one point, he turned to force a smile in Polly's direction, but her eyes were closed and the expression on her face was a pained grimace. Lily blew him a kiss, though, and he mouthed "I love you" before turning back to Huff's damning narrative.

In addition to displaying documents suggesting The Boss wasn't all-White, that he was having manliness problems, that his rallies were packed with paid seat-warmers, that senior aides were hiding advanced degrees, and that the League had a sex-trafficking problem, Huff showed the jury copies of two other documents that had made their way to the Web. One purported to show that the regime was secretly funneling subsidies to The Boss's favorite Boss Billionaires even as their accountants concocted massive tax breaks with artful financial engineering. Another was a supposedly genuine internal memo from the Good Food Administration reporting that last year's deadly salmonella outbreak among schoolchildren didn't originate in Pacifica's lettuce fields, as publicly reported, but at a Midwestern processing plant supplying beef to Burger Czar. Those rounded out the seven counts of slander, and Huff described each one of them with disgust and disdain.

When the stage was turned over to Wild Bill, he pulled his fragile frame out from behind the defense table and stood for a moment to conspicuously reveal his black, high-top basketball sneakers. Dash and LeBeau were wearing the same shoes because Wild Bill had delivered two pairs to the jail and insisted, without explanation, that they show up in court wearing the sneakers with their blue prison jumpsuits.

In a phlegmy old-man voice, and with arthritic hands clasped behind his bent back, Wild Bill flapped his eyebrows and announced, "The defense calls Izzy Andruzzi."

How Wild Bill had managed to land Andruzzi as a witness was a mystery to his clients. Dash had seen the barrel-chested, sixty-six-year-old comedian scores of times on late-night BTV, delivering raunchy, profane monologues whose topics ranged from renderings of the best way to change a flat tire on a tractor to his dirty-old-man escapades during wakes. LeBeau had heard of Andruzzi, but being stuck in Sanctuary Thirteen so long without BTV privileges led him to believe the comic was dead.

While Andruzzi stepped forward, Wild Bill leaned back toward Dash and whispered: "I appealed to his vanity. Told him he'd have the biggest BTV audience of his life and that he was so popular The Boss wouldn't dare throw him in jail, which of course might not be true. We'll see."

Andruzzi looked amused at the whole scene as he settled into the witness stand in his signature performance attire: dark gray slacks and a gray blazer over a black turtleneck that bulged from too many burgers and martinis. Seated in the raised witness stand, his chin was high as he scanned the courtroom like a potentate preparing for an audience with his supplicants. Dash and LeBeau immediately understood why they and Wild Bill were wearing black sneakers: Andruzzi was wearing the exact same high-tops. It was an element of his stage persona, and without saying a word, Wild Bill had managed to signal to the jury that they were all on the same team.

"State your name, please, for the record."

"Massimo Gianluca DiVicenza, but my stage name is Izzy Andruzzi. You can call me Izzy."

"How long have you been a comedian, sir?"

"They tell me I was cracking jokes in the womb."

"And when was your first professional gig?"

"I was, what, fourteen."

"So you've been a professional comedian for more than half a century. How many times would you say you've performed on BTV?"

"Maybe eighty. Roughly."

"And how many bitdollars have you earned in your career in comedy?"

"I live comfortably, Mr. Abrams. Three Bentleys and twenty-five cashmere turtlenecks. That draw a picture for you?"

"It does. Won any awards, sir?"

"Too many to count. You know, a few Grammys, a couple of Tonys, a Golden Globe, let's see, a Thurber, a Chortle in London, one in Italy I can't recall, and of course a Bossy."

"The Bossy, yes. And that was awarded by one of your biggest fans, right?"

"Acton Grudge, yes. Right in the Do It Room."

Wild Bill turned to Fullwood. "Your honor, I submit Mr. Andruzzi as an expert on comedy."

"Objection!" cried Huff. "Mr. Abrams is making a mockery of our entire system of justice. Slander, sedition, and treason are deadly serious charges, Your Honor!"

Wild Bill's eyebrows beat whomp-whomp-whomp like a pair of swans taking off from the surface of a lake. He replied slowly and with determination, arms spread wide, as if to signal Judge Fullwood that this was a make-or-break moment in his defense. "Here's what's deadly serious, Your Honor: a person's inability to take a joke. Being so thin-skinned and snippety that you can't laugh at yourself, at the absurdity of life, at the human condition, at all our vices and shortcomings. The phrase 'comic relief' exists for a reason. In the darkest times — and we've all lived them — comedy is a one-hundred-percent effective remedy. Our witness is going to characterize these documents in a manner that undermines the prosecution's entire case. That's why Mr. Huff is objecting so strenuously. If anyone knows what's funny and what's not, Izzy Andruzzi does, and his expert testimony needs to be heard, or the only thing that will be a mockery, as Mr. Huff puts it so contemptuously, is this very trial!"

"Objection overruled," Fullwood said impatiently in Huff's direction. "Mr. Andruzzi can testify, and the jury can decide."

The prosecutor's face was flushed and red, his ears the color of radishes. He sat back down in a steaming, defeated funk.

"Now, Izzy, let's look together at the so-called evidence." Wild Bill's voice was full of gravel. "Will you take a look at this spreadsheet listing advanced university degrees among high-ranking officials of the regime and tell me what ..." Bill had to stop right there. Izzy, spreadsheet in hand, was already bent over and laughing out loud. His body heaved. One hand gripped the front rail of the witness stand. The laughter started with a low he-he-he and built to a crescendo of loud guffaws, rolling cackles, and intermittent roars. By then, the jurors were either smiling uncontrollably or covering their mouths to stifle giggles.

Fullwood was trying his best to keep a straight face. Once he controlled himself, he turned to the witness. "Mr. Andruzzi, could you just answer the question?"

Izzy dialed back slowly and his mouth gently closed. "Oh, my God," he said, wiping tears from the sides of both wrinkled eyes. "What was the question again?"

"Do you find this spreadsheet funny, Izzy?" Wild Bill asked.

"I took one..." Izzy's belly started shaking again, but he covered his mouth and stifled his amusement. "Oooooh, okay, yes, well. Mr. Abrams, I took one look and had to laugh because here are brilliant people trying to look stupid and clueless by hiding their degrees. Ironic, right? That we want a government of morons, a race to the bottom? What's the opposite of meritocracy? I think it's idiocracy, right? I can see the job interview now. 'How many years have you been an idiot?' 'I can't count that high.' 'Okay, you're hired!'"

Huff was beside himself with rage, shaking his head and feverishly taking notes.

"In your expert opinion, Izzy," Wild Bill asked, "is this document a serious attempt to sabotage and collapse our current regime or maybe to poke fun at it?"

"It's not a nuclear warhead, for heck's sake. It's burlesque."

Wild Bill turned toward Huff as he walked back to his seat. "No further questions."

Fullwood cleared his throat. "Cross-examination, Mr. Huff."

George Remington Huff looked confused for a moment, like he was searching the air for a nuisance bug and finally found it. He rose.

"Mr. Andruzzi, have you ever been placed in a false light in front of millions of people?"

"Sure. Like ridiculed? When that happens, you punch back. Audiences love that."

"I don't mean ridiculed like ha-ha-that's-funny, but portrayed *falsely*. Let me give you an example. What if I leaked to BTV News a fake document showing you failed to pay taxes for five straight years? You'd be angry, wouldn't you?"

"Heck, yeah. But I've been called all kinds of shit by all kinds of people, and I don't go around demanding they be thrown into jail."

An unruly murmur arose from the audience, causing Fullwood to bang his gavel and threaten to clear the courtroom of visitors. Dash elbowed LeBeau, and Wild Bill sent a quick smile over his shoulder to Polly and Lily. Polly winked at him.

Huff retreated to his seat, emitting a barely audible "no further questions."

That's pretty much the way it went for most of the evidence introduced by the prosecution. Wild Bill would ask if a document was a serious attempt to topple Acton Grudge or just a bit of fun, and Izzy would break out laughing. Shoulders and bellies inside the jury box would start shaking and hands went over mouths. A few handkerchiefs would emerge to wipe away tears. Huff would try his best to steer everyone back to somber territory and note how nasty the documents were, how malicious and hurtful.

Izzy's reaction was decidedly more muted when Wild Bill asked about the purported sex trafficking inside the League of Christian Voters. "Now, that's what I'd call only borderline funny, worth about one snicker," the comedian testified. "You can definitely get laughs talking about sex, but sex trafficking? That's risky, you know?"

"Fair enough," said Wild Bill. "But tell me this, Izzy, why in the world would The Boss think a supposed revelation about sex trafficking inside the League slanders *him?*"

"You'd think the League might be more pissed off about it than the regime — unless the League was supplying..."

"Objection!" Huff screamed as he exploded out of his chair.

"Sustained," barked Fullwood. He turned to Izzy. "You're not an expert in sex trafficking, Mr. Andruzzi."

Wild Bill continued. "Alright Izzy, let me ask this: could there be *anything* funny about sex trafficking?"

"In certain contexts, yes," said Izzy. "Think about the irony. Strait-laced, God-fearing Christian voters who turn out to be dirty old men? That's pretty funny. Maybe it's two snickers instead of one."

On cross-examination, Huff managed to take Izzy down a notch or two, asking the comedian if he knew what sex trafficking meant, how common it was, the gangs involved, the international bans on forced labor, and the like. Izzy knew diddly-squat and got a little sheepish about it. Izzy was wincing and Huff was gloating as Fullwood offered Wild Bill an opportunity to clarify any testimony on re-direct.

Just then, a courtroom Enforcer escorted someone right up to Wild Bill's table, a poorly attired and sweaty man with a set of files under his arm. The two men whispered and gesticulated for more than a minute right in front of Dash and LeBeau before Judge Fullwood asked impatiently: "May we continue now, Mr. Abrams?"

Wild Bill approached Fullwood's bench and motioned Huff to join them. More whispering ensued until Fullwood announced that court would break for the day. He instructed Huff and Abrams to join him for a private conference in his chambers. Before leaving the courtroom, Wild Bill huddled with Dash and LeBeau. His eyebrows were flapping a mile a minute.

"Boys, we just may have the damn biggest break imaginable. Can't discuss the details til I talk to the judge, but you remember I hired an investigator? That was him. He's dug up a friggin' gold mine. And if Fullwood will allow it into evidence — and I think he's got to — we're gonna have ourselves one helluva trial, and it ain't gonna be based on testimony from a comedian."

"What's going on?" LeBeau asked insistently.

"All I can say is get ready to break out the hot buttered popcorn."

9

When George Huff delivered the bad news to Hector Saletan that the trial was taking a two-week recess so both sides could examine explosive new evidence about The Boss, the fixer exploded in foaming vitriol.

"Tell me you're lying!" Saletan shouted. "Tell me you're making this up, you little shit! This can't be, dammit! Jesus Fucking Christ!"

Huff took a step back and winced. "I know."

"You don't know shit! Listen to me!"

Saletan decelerated and exhaled slowly. His voice dropped sixty decibels. He looked down, his hands were at his temples. After a moment gathering himself, he looked back at Huff.

"I had a suspicion," he explained as he started pacing the room, "that there were grains of truth in some of those goddamn documents dumped on the Dark Web. It was a hunch, okay? I know The Boss inside out and some of it just rang true. The docs on the Web were fake, alright. It's just that when I told the BBI to track everything down to the last speck of dust, they came back to me not with grains of truth but boulders. Can you guess?"

"No, sir."

"Of course you can't, you dumb-ass!" Saletan was back in flame-thrower mode, and he enunciated each word for effect. "According to the BBI, a bunch of people in this government really *are* hiding their advanced degrees! They really *do* have secret fucking PhDs! And get this. The BBI discovered that The Boss's event team really *has been* stacking the Freedom Assemblies with paid attendees."

Huff, mouth agape, was speechless. Saletan filled the void.

"The goddamn BBI, at *my* insistence, found out that The Boss really *is* being treated for erectile dysfunction. You got that? And that he's *not* a hundred percent White! Is it registering yet?"

"Oh, shit."

"Yeah. Oh, shit. And get this, junior lawman. The fucking League really *is* being investigated for sex trafficking. And the salmonella outbreak really *did* start at the meat packing plant. And The Boss really *is* sweeping subsidies into the pockets of his favorite CEOs. All those fucking documents point straight to the truth. Have I spelled it out for you?"

"Yes, sir," Huff replied.

"You're damn right I have! So what did I do? I *immediately* put those BBI files in my safe, and someone inside *this* office must have leaked them to Wild Bill's private investigator. Either that, or there's a high-level spy inside the BBI. You see? You gettin' this picture, boy? Those are the only two places those reports existed. That goddamn private eye just sat in his office and jerked off while someone — I'll wring their fucking necks — copied the files and handed them over to Wild Bill Abrams & Company. Probably for a suitcase full of cash. You see it now? You see it?"

"I see it. But are the documents real, then?"

"Hell, no, they're not real!"

Huff was completely flummoxed.

"Then how did Dash Askin and Clary LeBeau know all that beforehand? How did they know to make fake documents about *real* situations and *real* events? That's the part I don't understand."

"How the fuck do I know!" Saletan sneered. "Either Askin's a fucking genius or he had inside information from the start. We're gonna turn this place upside down until we find out who leaked this shit and whether Askin was tipped off somehow. In the meantime, you gotta stall, Huff. You hear me? Stall as long as you can. We need time to figure this shit out. Delay the trial! We gotta get a cover story out there, so get back to the judge, make up some story, and deny, deny, deny. But get it delayed. You understand?"

"I don't know if I can stall Judge Fullwood...."

"Fuck Judge Fullwood, Huff! Stall the goddamn thing! No fucking excuses!"

W ild Bill Abrams met with Dash and LeBeau in a sweltering, barely furnished visitor room at Upstream Penitentiary, an hour's drive from Richard Fullwood's courtroom along concrete highways flanked by concrete apartment blocks and red-white-and-blue billboards announcing "Jesus and The Boss Love America." He carried a cardboard box full of manila folders housing copies of reports and memoranda from the Boss Bureau of Investigation that were never supposed to see the light of day. Hector Saletan had ordered the BBI investigations so he could know for himself what the public was never meant to know. He wanted to make sure his hunches were wrong, but if they turned out to be right, he needed a plan to squash dead any eight-legged little factoids that might crawl out into the public domain and reflect poorly on The Boss.

"How'd we get hold of these files?" Dash asked Wild Bill. "How do we know they're real? What if they just deny everything?"

"Keep your voices down, boys, because I guarantee you these walls have ears." Wild Bill leaned in and whispered. "We got 'em because the Underground has cash to offer in return for information, and people are naturally greedy. My investigator may look like a schmuck, but he is well-connected. All he did was put out the word on the street that we were interested in knowing certain things and willing to pay top bitdollar. We expected some scraps but not this glittering trove."

Le Beau whispered back, "But they're gonna call 'em fake, right? That's gotta be their strategy. Always is. Anything true is fake. Anything fake is true."

"I can't tell you boys just yet how we're gonna prove they're real, but you gotta trust me that we're not without weapons. And I'm gonna use every one of them."

"We better not be shooting blanks," Dash said glumly.

LeBeau couldn't contain his confusion. "How in heck did Dash pick Royal Fuckings that turned out to be true? He picked shit that might be plausible, but this? It's like we put a nickel of pure speculation into a one-armed bandit and rung up straight cherries and a gusher of quarters every time. I can't get my head around that."

Dash muttered, "Pure luck." But Wild Bill placed a fatherly hand on Dash's forearm to stop him.

"I know it may look like it," Wild Bill said, "but Dash ain't the clairvoyant he may think he is or that we might wish he was."

"Amen," said Dash. "I have no fucking idea how this happened."

"But you *do* know, Dash," Wild Bill responded. "You *do* know. You just don't realize it. I've been watching Bossism spread like a deadly virus from before The Boss took control, and the one thing I've learned is that these people are highly predictable. When you know someone's corrupt and ignorant and greedy and a liar, it's not hard to figure out what they're gonna do. Corrupt, greedy people steal and try to line their pockets. Ignorant people make stupid decisions. Liars lie. They try to cover shit up and distract, and they do it badly. If they say they're womanizing studs, there's a good chance they're impotent. If they tell you time and again that they're just common folk helping the God-fearing working class, it's a good bet they're filthy rich elitists. If they get all up in arms about pedophilia and birth control for sixteen-year-olds, you can bet there are sexual creeps in their midst. It's the smart people who are hard to judge, the clever ones who hide who they really are, the crafty ones who pretend in sophisticated ways and get away with it. These people here? The Boss's crowd? They are right up front. No surprises at all. What you see is what you get. And when they *do* try to hide something, they're just bad at it, totally transparent, inept. I'm guessing Dash was just imagining what these creeps *might* do and how they *might* be operating to come up with believable shit that he could exploit. When you know who people really are, and you try to imagine what's going on behind the scenes, you're gonna imagine shit that is *damned close to the truth*, and sometimes, as is the case here, it's *completely fuckin' true*. It's a rarity, alright, but a hundred-year flood never happens til it happens."

"Now that you say it out loud...," LeBeau mused. And Dash finished his sentence.

"...It sounds so plausible. Some of those ideas were mine but some came from our resident screenwriter and the public health shrink. They deserve the credit more than I do. I was mystified by it all. I even began to think there is a God and I'm his Chosen Servant. You know, Jesus delusions. Walking on water. Twilight Zone. But it's just probability, isn't it?"

"Your gift, Dash, is that you *understand* these crazy people. And you knew when the other DLs came up with ideas, they were smart ones that you could run with," Wild Bill continued. "You all could see right through the Boss mindset. And what you thought you *might* find turned out to be what was there. It wasn't such a big leap."

"But does this mean we're not going to prison?" LeBeau asked Wild Bill.

"Wish I could say that, Clary. In fact, it might make the sedition and treason charges all the more menacing. You see, when we prove in that courtroom that what you dished onto the Dark Web was the truth, the slander charges deflate and disappear. Unfortunately, those same documents now point to facts that are state secrets, and when you reveal state secrets meant to be held in confidence for so-called national security reasons — that's running close to treason, because they get to define what national security is."

"So, on the flip side, if The Boss and his people deny this stuff in the BBI reports," Dash theorized, "we might be acquitted of treason because it was all a joke. And then convicted of slander. But if we prove the BBI reports are true, we might slip out of the slander charges but strengthen their treason case because it was never supposed to come to light?"

"Sadly, that's right."

"What about the malice issue, Wild Bill?" LeBeau asked.

"That's a harder one to predict. If the jury believes the stuff in the documents is true, they and the judge will have a big hand in deciding if the secrets were damaging and were revealed maliciously or all in good fun."

"We're fucked," LeBeau concluded.

"Yeah, we're cooked," Dash added.

"Just hold on a minute," Wild Bill cautioned. "We have some wedges to exploit. We have angles to mine. We have ways to put ideas out there. We have theories. We have a can of gray paint to splash all over the black and white that young Mr. Huff is gonna throw onto the wall. That's what defense lawyers do, boys, and I've been at it a long, long time. You plant doubt."

The meeting ended pretty much where it began, with a few faint rays of hope trying to penetrate the surface of a bog full of muck.

Despite Hector Saletan's ultimatum to George Huff, Judge Fullwood was not in a buying mood when the prosecutor put before him five reasons to delay the sensational trial of Dashiel Askin and Clary LeBeau. When Huff broke the bad news to Saletan in a phone call, The Boss's fixer veered into full intimidation mode, just as Huff had anticipated.

"You're a candy-ass pussy of a prosecutor, Huff, and I'm gonna have your job. You hear that? You're weak. You're disloyal. You're a fuck-up. You're not as smart as you think. You're an arrogant little snot-nosed legal weakling masquerading as some kind of Andrew Jackson. Don't even bother to return to Fullwood's courtroom, Huff. I'm getting a new prosecutor. A *real* prosecutor. Pick up your last paycheck and get out!"

That was the end of George Remington Huff's legal career. When the trial resumed, a new prosecutor was in Huff's chair, Anna Maria Fabulini, a young aide to The Boss who departed the regime's employ to attend law school and subsequently joined the staff of The Boss's Chief Law and Order Officer. She had introduced herself to Fullwood and Wild Bill in the judge's chambers the day before, and Wild Bill took it as a good sign that she was now on the case. The prosecution was obviously wobbling on a thin sheet of ice that was starting to crack.

When court finally resumed, Fullwood lowered his gavel and addressed the jury:

"Ladies and gentlemen, Mr. Huff has taken ill and will not be able to continue presenting the government's case in this matter. He's not seriously ill but incapacitated for the moment, and we wish him a speedy recovery. The government case will be presented by Miss Fabulini. You have the floor, counsel."

Fabulini looked like a BTV soap opera version of a female lawyer. She wore an immaculately tailored navy blue suit over a white blouse, killer high heels, and fiery lipstick. Wild Bill knew her as an aggressive prosecutor and a worthy adversary, and he decided he would treat her with the utmost respect while trying to eviscerate her case.

"Your Honor," said Fabulini, "the government moves for an order of inadmissibility regarding the so-called new evidence in this case. On its face, this evidence is without any basis in fact and must be barred from this trial."

Fullwood motioned to her and Wild Bill to step up to the bench, and the three of them engaged in an animated discussion during which Wild Bill assured the judge that he had *proof* the new evidence wasn't fabricated hogwash. The judge uttered an audible "alright" and sent them back to their respective tables. Fabulini felt ambushed and looked disturbed.

Dash whispered to Wild Bill. "What'd you tell him?"

"That we can prove our case, what else?"

"How?"

"Watch."

Fullwood cleared his throat. "Alright, Miss Fabulini, I'm going to rule the new evidence admissible based on the assertions of the defense counsel. He now has the burden of bringing forth the material he claims to possess. The jury will decide as to its veracity. Now, does the government have a witness?"

"First, Your Honor," Fabulini said, "I ask that you declare a mistrial."

An exasperated Fullwood mumbled, "Denied. Do you have a witness, Miss Fabulini?"

"Yes. The prosecution calls Mr. Ray Miller, Director of the Boss Bureau of Investigation."

The courtroom buzzed as the salt-and-pepper-haired Miller strode purposefully to the witness stand, folded his reading glasses, and slipped them into the breast pocket of his lime green suit jacket.

Fabulini gave him a welcome smile. "Mr. Miller, would you look over these pages of purported BBI reports and memoranda and tell the jury whether any of them look genuine?"

Miller reached for his glasses and flipped through the pages rapidly, as if they were out-of-date train schedules.

"These are obviously fake, fraudulent, counterfeit forgeries, all of them," he replied. "I have never seen them before in my life." He sent a smile of satisfaction in Wild Bill's direction.

"And beyond the question of their authenticity, Mr. Miller, would you tell the jury, so far as you know, if *any* of the *alleged* facts that these documents *purport* to show are true?"

"I'm not sure I get the question. You mean, like, does The Boss actually have erectile dysfunction?"

Fullwood felt Fabulini's pain and intervened. "It's a yes or no question, Mr. Miller."

Miller was red-faced, realizing his error. He thought he might have just lost his job. He gathered himself and said in a near whisper, "No. Nothing is true."

"No further questions."

Now Wild Bill went to work. He'd swapped the black sneakers for worn out brogues. He seemed to be standing more erect. His eyebrows didn't move. He demonstrably smoothed his tie and cleared his throat as if the Queen of England was about to stride into the courtroom.

"The defense calls Mr. George Remington Huff."

Fabulini sat stunned, then rocketed out of her chair. "Objection! The government has not been informed of this witness!"

"We just learned this morning, Your Honor, that this individual is willing to testify," Wild Bill lied. He'd known for a week that Huff was a deeply embittered man and was ready to turn on The Boss and Hector Saletan, even if it jeopardized his freedom.

Dash elbowed LeBeau, turned, and whispered, "How the hell did he pull that rabbit out of his hat?"

"No fuckin' idea, but I ain't complaining."

Fullwood took another moment of whispering at the bench with the two attorneys. The judge's eyebrows nearly hit the ceiling and Fabulini's head fell to her chest when Wild Bill told them what Huff was going to say under oath. Wild Bill turned and motioned Huff to come forward from the back of the courtroom. He was dressed like he was headed to a suburban wedding to serve as Best Man, just without the boutonniere.

"We'll hear from the witness," Fullwood announced.

Thereupon, Wild Bill launched one of his most glorious courtroom moments. First, he led Huff through his education and background, then the timeline of his being assigned the case, his stormy meeting with Hector Saletan, and his abrupt removal as prosecutor. Fabulini moved to strike Huff's description of the meeting with Saletan as hearsay, but Fullwood overruled her, saying she was free to put Hector Saletan himself on the stand.

Wild Bill asked: "And how did it *feel*, Mr. Huff, to be *bounced* as prosecutor on the phone after such an *illustrious* career, as if you were a *hick* who didn't know *shit from Shinola*? Did you feel like you'd been *betrayed* by people you worshiped but who turned out to be frauds and fools?"

"Objection!" Fabulini stormed, slamming her palm on the prosecutor's table.

"Sustained. Watch it, Mr. Abrams," Fullwood cautioned. "Do not lead the witness. The jury will disregard the question."

"Certainly, Your Honor. I'll rephrase. How did it feel to be fired, son?"

"You know, it felt shitty. It was wrong. It was unwarranted. It felt like I'd been betrayed by people I worshipped who turned out to be frauds and fools."

Head down, Fullwood rubbed his brow. Fabulini's jaw fell open. Wild Bill's eyebrows fluttered.

"And deep in your soul, Mr. Huff, you wanted the truth to come out, didn't you."

"I did."

"And you telephoned me."

"I did."

"And you told me what Hector Saletan imparted to you, in a somewhat *colorful* fashion."

"I did."

"That *every one* of the allegations behind the documents that launched this unfortunate prosecution is *true*. Is that right, sir?"

"Objection!" Fabulini yelled. "Hearsay!"

"Overruled."

"I did, Mr. Abrams. Just like you said. That's what Mr. Saletan told me. He said the BBI found they were all true."

"Now, Mr. Huff, please tell the jury why in the world they should take your word for this. Why should the court believe that a witness who's been cut down from his job as prosecutor in this very case and humiliated — why should that person be believed when he describes comments allegedly made by this country's longtime Chief Cleansing Officer, Hector Saletan?"

"Ordinarily, such a witness should not be believed, sir."

"Should *not* be believed?"

"No, sir."

"Except when...what, Mr. Huff?"

"Except when the witness has a videotape of the entire meeting."

All hell broke loose in Richard Fullwood's courtroom. Fabulini's shouts of "objection!" were drowned out by gasps and murmurs from the audience, Dash Askin's hand slamming onto the surface of the defense table, Clary LeBeau's loud "No shit!", and Fullwood's gavel repeatedly thundering down onto its varnished oak base.

"Order!" Fullwood shouted. "Order!"

"Is the popcorn hot?" LeBeau whispered to Dash.

At that very moment, the on-duty censor at BTV headquarters six-hundred miles away awakened to the realization that the network might be about to show tens of millions of viewers a video of Hector Saletan blasting Prosecutor George Huff in an epithet-laden tirade — during which Saletan would confirm that all of the alleged slander against The Boss was true because that's what the BBI had discovered.

The censor flipped a large red toggle switch on his console, immediately shutting down live trial coverage and shunting the program to an archived recording of Beethoven's Ninth Symphony by the Berlin Philharmonic under the baton of Herbert von Karajan. He phoned BTV headquarters, explained the situation, and waited for a special message to begin scrolling across the bottom of the symphony screen. The message began rolling: "Due to technical difficulties, we are unable to resume live coverage of the slander, sedition, and treason trial of the Deranged Lunatics Dashiel Askin and Clary LeBeau."

When the tumult inside the courtroom died down, George Huff stated that he had recorded his conversation with Hector Saletan on his phone, which was in his hand through the entire encounter, video lens facing outward to the gesticulating Chief Cleansing Officer. Huff then handed his phone to Wild Bill, who plugged it into a video monitor rolled out near the judge and jury, then tapped on the video's start arrow. Saletan's voice and image were stunningly clear. Nobody so much as twitched in Fullwood's courtroom.

When it was over, Wild Bill moved for a directed verdict of acquittal on all counts, arguing that truth was a valid defense in a defamation case.

"Objection," Fabulini said with a sigh. "Your Honor, these defendants were clearly disseminating damaging information, private information, classified information, personal information with profound malice, willfully, and with the intention of bringing our government down. That is slander and that is sedition and, yes, that is treason."

"Mr. Abrams," Fullwood asked, "are you suggesting that the testimony of Izzy Abruzzi about all of this being a joke should be stricken from the record?"

"No, sir! Not at all. I would argue that true statements can be amusing if they are shocking, absurd, and inexplicable. But as to the question of a directed verdict, we have heard and seen credible testimony that my clients were not disseminating falsehoods."

Fullwood dismissed the jury for the day and took two hours in his chambers to think about Wild Bill's request for a directed verdict of not guilty, an hour of which was consumed by a contentious back and forth between Anna Maria Fabulini and William Abrams.

When the trial resumed the next day, Fullwood called in the jury and explained why he was going to direct a verdict of not guilty only on the slander charges and resume testimony as to whether the sedition and treason charges were valid based on the defendants' intent.

It was a bittersweet moment at the defense table.

"They got to him," Wild Bill whispered to his clients, his bitterness evident. "He's been told to put you guys in prison, no matter what."

"I thought it's up to the jury," Dash offered.

"Fullwood holds all the cards. He's gonna explain the law before they deliberate, and he can do that in ways that plant the desired outcome in the jury's mind."

"We're fucked," said LeBeau.

Fullwood gave Fabulini the floor. Glancing at Wild Bill with a look of cool contentment, she said, "The defense calls Mr. Caleb Jones."

Caleb walked slowly to the witness stand, eyes cast toward the floor. He turned toward the defense table briefly and mouthed the words "I'm sorry." Dash mouthed back, "It's okay."

Fabulini walked Caleb through his employment record at Sanctuary Thirteen and instructed him to explain how and why he began working with the Underground.

"I got confused and thought they were good people. I wanted to befriend them and I wanted them to be my friend," Caleb testified, "but I think they took advantage of that friendship."

Dash was in pain, not because Caleb's words stung but because he knew his vengeful desire to hurt The Boss from inside Sanctuary Thirteen had set in motion potentially damaging events he could not control. He didn't believe Caleb was truly hurt, though. Instead, he saw a man wounded by circumstances over which he had no control.

Fabulini asked: "Did the defendants discuss their plan to build an unauthorized communication device?"

"Yes."

"And did you help them create that device by providing a battery, which was not an item employees were permitted to bring into the Sanctuary?"

"Yes, ma'am."

"Now, did the defendants tell you why they needed a battery?"

"They said they needed it for a Royal Fucking."

"And did they describe what they were planning?"

"No. Just said a Royal Fucking. I knew what that was."

"And did they tell you who was going to be the target of this scheme?"

"No, but I knew it was meant for The Boss."

"How did you know that?"

"Boss Haters know what other Boss Haters are up to. You know, they hate The Boss."

"And did you think the defendants were Boss Haters?"

"Everyone at Thirteen is."

"Are you a Boss Hater, Mr. Jones?"

"Not anymore. No ma'am. Blessed Be The Boss."

"Let's get back to what you call a Royal Fucking. Would you tell the court what a Fucking means to you."

"It's when, you know, when you screw someone."

"And what do you mean by screw?"

"You know, fuck over."

"And what does fuck over mean?"

Fullwood had had enough. "Mr. Jones, you are resorting to tautology, so I'm going to ask you to define the phrase Miss Fabulini asked about *without* repeating that same word or similar words."

"You mean Royal Fucking?"

Fullwood's eyes closed slowly. "Yes, that phrase."

"Yes, sir, Your Honor. I'll try. Royal Fucking means hurting someone or taking advantage of them."

"Or abusing them?" Fabulini asked.

"Yeah, I guess."

"Or cheating them?"

"I guess."

"Or manipulating them?"

"Maybe. Yes, ma'am."

"Thinking about all these definitions, would you say there is likely to be malice or willful intent to harm behind any urge to deliver a Royal Fucking?"

"I guess so."

Fabulini was done, and Wild Bill stepped forward. Caleb removed a handkerchief from his pocket and wiped his brow. Dash tried to catch his eye so he could somehow convey his empathy.

"I want to talk some more about definitions, Mr. Jones. Did you ever hear the term 'fucked up?'" Wild Bill asked.

Fabulini objected but Fullwood allowed the question.

"Sure, I've heard of 'fucked up'."

"And what does that mean to you?"

"Well, messed up or confused or discombobulated."

"Is there intentional harm behind that?"

"Not necessarily."

"Did you ever hear the term 'fucked up' with reference to overindulgence in drugs or alcohol?" Wild Bill's eyebrows fluttered.

"Yes, sir. It means drunk or high."

"And is there intentional harm behind that?"

"Don't think so."

"Now Mr. Jones, could a Fucking or a Royal Fucking be a prank?"

"Sure could. Yes, sir."

"And is there malice or intentional harm behind a prank?"

"Not really. It's all in fun."

"And when the defendants told you they needed the battery for a Royal Fucking, you reacted in a specific way, didn't you, Mr. Jones."

"I guess so, yeah."

"And what way was that?"

"I laughed. Dash and LeBeau are two funny dudes. Pranksters."

"You laughed."

"Yes, sir."

"Mr. Jones, I want to turn to another topic, which is how you got to this witness stand. Did you sign an agreement with the prosecutor to testify against the defendants in return for your freedom under a suspended sentence?"

"Yes, I did."

"And when the BBI questioned you, did you agree to tell them everything you knew right from the start? Or did the BBI offer you any inducements or threaten you at all, or threaten your family to get you to provide information about the defendants?"

"Objection!" Fabulini cried.

"Sustained. Mr. Abrams, you are out of bounds."

From the fourth row of audience seats, an elderly woman rose and shouted while pointing a shaking finger at Judge Fullwood. Abrams turned. Fabulini turned. Dash and LeBeau turned. Polly and Lily turned.

"Out of bounds?" the woman screamed. "Out of bounds? That question ain't out of bounds, Judge! Caleb was threatened, alright! They threatened him and threatened me and my child and my child's husband and my child's child! They're goons! They use coercion!"

On the witness stand, Caleb was in shock. He repeated over and over, "Agnes, sit down! Sit down!"

Fullwood hammered his gavel while two Court Enforcers strode from the back of the courtroom and pulled Agnes Jones out into the aisle. Her hands were shaking.

"Bullies!" she yelled as they hustled her out of the courtroom. "Thugs!"

When quiet returned, Fullwood instructed the jurors to ignore the outburst, cautioned Wild Bill again, and asked Caleb if he was calm enough to continue testifying.

"I guess," he replied, wiping his face again with the handkerchief.

Abrams continued. "Was that your wife, Mr. Jones?"

"Objection," Fabulini said in a weary tone.

"Overruled. You may answer, Mr. Jones."

"Yes, sir. She is a good woman. A brave woman. A..."

"That's enough, Mr. Jones," Fullwood interrupted. "You've answered the question."

Abrams turned toward the defense table. "No further questions, Your Honor."

Bombast and feigned outrage dominated the closing argument delivered by Anna Maria Fabulini. She spent two hours shoveling a grievance-filled rationale at the jury while Wild Bill repeatedly objected to her mischaracterizations of the evidence. Fullwood's exasperation boiled but he mostly allowed the prosecutor to drive home the point that maliciously placing into the public arena embarrassing private information, whether true or not, undermined two indispensable pillars of Bossism: public order and government security. Therefore, she concluded, Dash and LeBeau had committed treasonous and seditious acts.

Wild Bill felt some admiration for Fabulini. She'd performed well. It was all great theater. And he knew he had a steep hill to climb. As the trial lurched toward a conclusion, Dash and LeBeau had lobbied to have Wild Bill use his closing argument not merely to sow doubt about their guilt but to continue delivering a Royal Fucking to the regime, using every opportunity to skewer The Boss. Even with the BTV camera crew gone, Dash was confident that a courtroom condemnation of the regime would leak quickly into the river of information that inundated the public every day. He and LeBeau felt so strongly about continuing the Royal Fucking that they told Wild Bill it would mean more to them than avoiding prison. While acquittal might be satisfying, it also meant returning in straitjackets to Sanctuary Thirteen as Deranged Lunatics.

"Ladies and gentlemen, there's something much more important happening in this courtroom than the trial of my clients," Wild Bill opened as he paced along the jury box railing, eyebrows aflutter. "More important than a computer engineer and an auto body repairman who wear the scarlet letter of Deranged Lunatic but were somehow sane enough to bring to light damning facts about our government that our leaders didn't want you to know. More important than how you define a Royal Straight Flush or Royal Straight Fucking. More important than whether Acton Grudge wets his pants when someone calls him a name."

Fullwood slammed his gavel down hard. "The jury will disregard the last remark. Mr. Abrams, any further rhetorical excursions into schoolyard taunts will result in a contempt order."

"Certainly, Your Honor. I got carried away. I've never really learned to restrain myself when matters as important as the nature of our civic life are concerned. Besides, I believe these fine jurors understand what I'm talking about when I say 'more important.' They may not agree. And if they did, they sure wouldn't admit it, because they fear what might happen to them if they thought the wrong thoughts, the inconvenient thoughts about what's going on here. My clients did something entirely fearless and unexpected. They poked fun at an important person. You could say they mocked him. They understood the type of person our leader is with such clarity that the actions and circumstances they *imagined*, lo and behold, turned out to be true. It won't happen again in a hundred years. Hypothetically, when you encounter a man as crooked as a dog's hind leg, you can predict certain things about that man's actions, can't you. When you identify, hypothetically now, a liar, you can predict what might be said or what might be left unsaid, what might be hidden from you. God forbid that you find a man thoroughly lacking in character and humanity, but if you do, you can easily predict scandal and malfeasance and misfeasance and cruelty. My clients aren't clairvoyant, ladies and gentlemen. They just used their brains and their common sense."

Wild Bill smoothed out his tie between sentences and flapped his eyebrows now and again. Each time he said "my clients," he turned and directed a gnarled pointer finger at Dash and LeBeau. When he said "They poked fun at an important person," he did so in a stage whisper.

"So, yes, they poked fun and maybe it drifted into mockery. But mockery, my friends, is not treason or sedition unless you happen to live in a totalitarian state. Poking fun and satirizing someone is not treason or sedition unless you live in a place like Russia under Joe Stalin. Now, that was a totalitarian state. And if you mocked Chairman Stalin, you could kiss your life goodbye and maybe the lives of your family. Is that what we do in the Land of the Free and the Home of the Brave? Do we throw people in prison for mockery when they actually tell us the truth? God, I hope not. Because that's barbaric and inhumane. They say the truth hurts. But is it malicious? Is the truth so harmful that you need to bus people up to the federal penitentiary and slam the door shut for forty years? No, it's not. I'll tell you why the truth sometimes hurts. It makes you sad. That's all. Just sad. It causes you to see more clearly, even if you don't like what you see. It allows you to venture outside your self-styled shell. It makes you see that the reality you believed in is flawed. And sometimes that's sad, because it's way easier to be a Passivist, to fool yourself, to live in a fantasy world where everything is great and no one goes hungry. Sounds appealing. But reality catches up to you. You can't escape it. And the reality here is that a powerful man with a tender ego felt so slighted, so embarrassed, so humiliated because my clients told the truth about him that he ordered up a trial for sedition and treason so he could practice more public brutality and therein give us all a lesson in the true meaning of Shut-up-ism and fear."

"You have been warned, Mr. Abrams," Fullwood said sternly.

"I'm wrapping up, Your Honor. Here's how I'll put this to you, ladies and gentlemen. If you truly believe that the unvarnished facts my clients revealed about the regime — your government, really, in a moment of inspired frivolity — if you believe those facts were so horrific and shameful and did irreparable harm to the security of our nation and our society, you go right ahead and send them back to the Upstream Penitentiary as quick as you can say the word 'to-tal-i-tarian.' But if you believe your country cannot be and should never become an instrument of oppression and arbitrariness and tyranny when ordinary citizens bring you the truth at great risk, why I would invite you to return a verdict of not guilty, go home, look yourself in the mirror, and know there are better days ahead."

10

The mutual respect between Richard Fullwood and William Abrams ran deep, but as he sat in his chambers the morning after closing arguments, listening to a Mozart piano concerto in the background while Wild Bill huffed about the perversion of language in the treason and sedition statutes, the judge felt his patience evaporating.

"We used to have a Constitution, Dickie."

"I do recall that, Bill."

"And it said what treason meant making war against us or adhering to our enemies."

"Giving them aid and comfort."

"Exactly so. But that changed, didn't it."

"Bill...."

"No, hear me out. It changed radically under Bossism. The sentences were lengthened to life in prison."

"I'm aware."

"And it got all muddied up with anti-terrorism laws — they used phrases like 'endangering lives' and 'destabilizing the nation'. They added the word "sabotage." They added this whole affiliation thing — affiliating with any organization involved in activities against the security of the nation, whatever the hell that means."

"I'm aware, Bill."

"The thing is, Dickie, we just bought the autocratic playbook. The Russians learned how to inject seemingly innocuous words into a law that made it so pliable that almost anyone minding his own business on a street corner in Moscow could be handcuffed and found guilty of terrible things. We copied Russia, and nobody said a goddamn word."

"I'm familiar with recent history, Bill."

"And maybe the worst of all was what they did to the sedition laws. They took out the words 'by force' and replaced them with 'coercion or intimidation.'"

"I do know that, Bill."

"Force means force, right? But what the hell do 'coercion and intimidation' mean? And if The Boss thinks you've said something intimidating or coercive, he can have you arrested. I don't know, maybe I'm intimidating you right now, Dickie."

"What's your point?"

"Hell, Dickie, my point is that we've slid straight into a world where freedom of speech is flat-out meaningless. Read the fucking Grudgments. 'Free Speech Is Without Limit; Malicious Dissent Is Not.' Now what the hell does that mean? It means any public official can charge just about anyone with using words he doesn't like and get all huffy about destabilizing the government. The Boss can charge my granddaughter, for God's sake, if she writes in the school paper that he's a bully. She tried to, and the teacher told her she couldn't write it. Too dangerous. Self-censorship reigns! And that was twenty years ago! It's only gotten worse."

"Come on, Bill. It's not as bad as you think."

"Well, heck, you know we're nothing like the country we used to be. We live in a dictatorship. Everyone lives in abject fear. We dig little holes for ourselves and climb in and hope the demons won't get us. We don't want to know what's happening outside our little hole, because if we did, we might have to do something about it, and Jesus Christ, that would be too much, too taxing, too demanding, and far too dangerous. Let someone else do it. Not me! Then, of course, The Boss's boys lean on people, and it's none too subtle. The propaganda. Look what they did to poor Caleb Jones. That was a man intimidated into testifying if I ever saw one. Plain as day. I wonder what they threatened him with. I bet they even lean on people like *you* once in a while, Judge, don't they?"

Bill's eyebrows were going fast and furious, as if they alone were trying to coax an answer out of Fullwood.

"I'm not going to get into that, Bill. That's out of bounds, and you know it. I asked you here to talk about how I'm going to explain the law to this jury before they deliberate. I don't need a harangue, and I didn't make the law you're bellyaching about. But if I want to keep my job, I do have to enforce it. And the jury does, too."

"You're bringing Fabulini in to talk, too, aren't you."

"Of course I am. It's a courtesy. I want to make sure I'm doing this right. That's what good judges do."

"What I'm saying, Dickie, is that the law is Grade A horse manure. It's been twisted so much the Founders of this country wouldn't recognize it. If The Boss calls you an Enemy of the People, he might as well be calling you a traitor. He can whip up a treason or sedition charge anytime he good and well pleases."

"And what I'm saying, Bill, is that I can't change the law."

"Do you stand for anything, Dickie? Do you stand for justice, even?" Bill was begging. He was in pain.

It took all of Fullwood's patience, compassion, and willpower to keep from exploding.

"I know you're hurting now, Bill. For your clients. Don't make it worse. I'm going to do my best to keep the definitions narrow. That's all I can do. If it was up to me, you'd be happily writing your memoirs in a cabin overlooking a forest stream somewhere, writing about an illustrious legal career and not what it was like to be sent to Sanctuary One and taught a lesson on Shut-up-ism. You know that. You probably don't believe it, but I admire you, Billie. I do. My job is to work within the law, though. And I do sleep at night."

There was a knock on the door, and one of Fullwood's young clerks stepped part-way in, holding up a folded piece of paper. Fullwood waved him in, and the clerk placed the note on the judge's desk.

"My god," Fullwood said, looking up. "Big news, Bill."

"Yeah?"

"Acton Grudge died of a heart attack this morning in the Do It Room. The First Physician confirmed it."

"What?"

"There's more. Boss Junior announced that the Board had named him Ultimate Boss."

Wild Bill slumped in his chair. His right hand was on his forehead, pressing, like something was trying to push through his skull and he had to keep it in.

"Hey, Billie, you okay?"

"Shit," said Wild Bill.

"I thought you'd be wildly happy. Your clients did this, you know. Their gambit worked. I heard there was a lot of hand-wringing on The Boss's team about the news coming out of this trial, and The Boss was infuriated. Your boys scared him to death. Do you see that?"

Wild Bill spoke calmly, quietly. "Maybe they did cause it. Who knows. But now the jury's gonna blame my clients for that wretched man's demise. Alright, I've said my piece."

He rose and picked up his briefcase.

"Bill..."

"Never mind, Dickie. Never mind."

Wild Bill walked out and shut the door behind him with a soft click.

That afternoon, after a moment of silence inside Judge Fullwood's courtroom for the memory of Acton Grudge, Fullwood announced that it was Boss Junior's wish to see a quick verdict and sentencing in the trial of the DL's Dash Askin and Clary LeBeau. No time for black crepe.

Everything that happened seemed subdued. Neither Dash nor LeBeau celebrated, because who could cheer the passing of the torch from one Caesar to another? If anything, Dash thought, Boss Junior was dumber and more dangerous than his late father.

Speaking calmly and slowly, Fullwood delivered a brief charge to the jury. He characterized treason as the more serious of the offenses and told the jury they would need to either find that the defendants made war against us or aided a foreign adversary in war or committed acts that "destabilized or sabotaged" the government. Thus, the jury would decide the question of whether The Boss embodied the government. Is the government thent us? Is it The Boss? Or is it some amorphous, faceless, interconnected, public conglomerate we all engage with from time to time? Fullwood never said, and Wild Bill took notice.

He also left to the jury the meanings of the words 'sabotage' and 'destabilize.' They would have the task of deciding if the facts that Dash and LeBeau disclosed to the public were inherently destructive.

Seditious conspiracy was another matter, and here, Fullwood had almost no room for nuance. Sedition, he said, means trying to overthrow, put down, or destroy the government by coercion or intimidation or oppose the authority of the government by coercion or intimidation, or prevent the execution of any law by coercion or intimidation. It would be up to them to define coercion or intimidation. The twelve jurors scribbled notes, and when Fullwood told them he would be available to answer any written questions, they all looked at each other like everything was as clear as a spring-fed mountain lake.

Over the next forty-five minutes, bailiffs served the jurors Boss Burgers and America Numero Uno coffee and reminded them that their Participation Payments would be wired directly to their bank accounts. They also deliberated, and when they let it be known that a unanimous verdict was reached, the bailiffs escorted Dash and LeBeau back into the courtroom from a secure holding room. Wild Bill shuffled in, bent over, and placed two gnarled hands on his clients' shoulders, and both men turned to smile at him.

"Can't fault anything you've done, Bill," Dash said.

"Yeah," said LeBeau. "You get my vote for the lawyer with the biggest balls."

"If it's any comfort to you," Wild Bill said, "Fullwood confided to me that he thinks you boys caused Grudge's heart failure."

"What do you think, Bill?" Dash inquired.

"It's probably true. You boys shook the whole kingdom."

"We weren't trying to kill the bastard," LeBeau offered. "We were trying to kill his regime, to kill the system, to end the corruption and stupidity."

"I'll admit I'm not unhappy The Boss is gone," said Dash. "Good riddance. But look what we got, Boss Junior. And he's now shining a bright light on this trial and this jury. We don't stand a chance."

Wild Bill whispered to both of them: "Either of you know the Latin phrase *dum spiro spero?*"

He drew blank stares.

"I always think of it when I'm waitin' for a verdict. It means "While I breathe, I hope."

Dash turned back toward his wife and daughter. Polly was gripping Lily's hand in both of hers, squeezing. Lily had her eyes closed tightly, like she was wishing on a star and had to block out every photon.

"All rise!" the bailiff shouted.

Fullwood sat down and asked that the jury be brought in.

"Ladies and gentlemen of the jury, have you reached a verdict?"

The foreman rose. "We have, Your Honor."

"On the count of treason, what say you?"

"Not guilty."

Dash and LeBeau slumped and Wild Bill whispered, "Lordy." Polly and Lily grabbed each other. Some in the audience shook their heads; one man shouted, "No!"

Fullwood banged his gavel once.

"Let's have quiet now. On the count of seditious conspiracy, what say you?"

The foreman seemed to hesitate ever so slightly.

"Guilty."

The audience erupted, and a few sped out the courtroom doors. Wild Bill's shoulders dropped. His eyebrows were still. Dash and LeBeau were as motionless as granite, staring straight ahead. Polly gasped, grabbed Lily's forearm, and held on until Lily's arm grew white.

Lily's face was contorted and she said, "Oh, please, please, please, please, please, please."

Dash's right hand was glued to LeBeau's arm. Fullwood looked first at Anna Maria Fabulini, who was smiling broadly. The judge offered a crisp, perfunctory nod. He then turned his gaze to Wild Bill Abrams, who by then had lifted his chin to look at the judge. Fullwood was pale and had a strained look on his face. He locked onto Wild Bill's eyes for what seemed like an eternity and finally lifted his eyebrows ever so slightly. Wild Bill responded with one brief flick of his own. It was over.

"I failed you boys," Wild Bill said as Dash wrapped an arm around his lawyer's shoulders.

Polly was sobbing and so was Lily. The great hubbub that had seized the courtroom began to quiet down. Fullwood was signing a few papers while Wild Bill and Fabulini started stuffing files and notes into their briefcases.

Then, an unmistakable chorus arose from outside on the street. It seemed like thousands of voices, were penetrating the courtroom windows. People must have filled the courthouse square, Dash thought. He heard them clearly, and it was beautiful.

"Amazing grace, how sweet the sound, that saved a wretch like me. I once was lost, but now am found. Was blind but now I see..." They sang so slowly and with such unity and force that Dash imagined a conductor standing on the courthouse steps urging them to deliver their very best with wide-open hands reaching to the heavens. The singing stopped after the third stanza: "Through many dangers, toils and snares, I have already come; 'Tis grace hath brought me safe thus far, and grace will lead me home..."

No one in the courtroom moved. A few voices inside had joined in, including Polly and Lily. Unashamed tears ran down the cheeks of Dash and LeBeau. Wild Bill let out a deep sigh and wiped his nose with a handkerchief.

When the hymn ended, Fullwood quieted everyone with four muted taps of his gavel.

"We'll schedule sentencing for Monday," he said. "Court is adjourned."

Fabulini walked out, joined by audience members offering congratulatory hugs and handshakes.

Dash stood and held Polly and Lily in a long, tearful embrace. Polly reached out and grasped Clary LeBeau's hand.

"Don't worry," LeBeau told her. "We're gonna walk outta here with our heads high."

The prison security guards kept a respectful distance until Dash released his family and turned away.

"It's time to go," one of the guards said.

On sentencing day, Dash and LeBeau sat silently in a courthouse holding room, staring out the window at a bright blue sky. There was nothing more to say. In the van ride from the jail, they had already talked about what they wanted to say when they addressed the court before sentencing. Neither of them had any intention of offering words of remorse.

"I just wanna show 'em they haven't changed one thing about me," LeBeau told Dash. "I'm the same ornery sumbitch who told 'em to shove it seven years ago."

"You're an amazing example," Dash told his friend. "I couldn't have gone through with this without you sitting beside me. Think of it, Clary, we knocked a dictator right off his pedestal. Trouble is, someone just like him climbed back up."

"No regrets, though?"

"None. I knew I'd be right here one day. Over the years, I kept telling myself: 'Just do what you said you'd do.' Oh, yeah, I had moments of doubt and real fear. I know what it's like to feel weak. And I couldn't have done anything if I thought Polly would crumble. She's been like iron, that woman. So I feel nothing but calmness today. An inner calm. Serenity. You know what I mean?"

"Hell, yes," LeBeau replied. "Same with me. My soul is satisfied."

Inside the holding room, LeBeau broke the silence.

"You gonna write me a letter or two from prison, I hope? It'll be like old times."

"Count on it," Dash replied.

A bailiff came in and motioned the two into the courtroom, where Wild Bill was waiting. The room was packed. Polly and Lily smiled as they held hands. It seemed to Dash that they, too, were at peace.

LeBeau addressed the court first, and in his own way, he was eloquent.

"No way was this regime or the one that comes after gonna break me, Your Honor. I've been put away for years now, and you'll never drain an ounce of regret out of me. I've always walked with my eyes open, guided by the truth, and I ain't stoppin' now. Someday, we're gonna wash away the stain of tyranny. I believe that. Until then, I'll never be a slave to Shut-up-ism. And, yeah, just one more thing. This is all bullshit."

"Thank you, Mr. LeBeau. And Mr. Askin, please?"

Dash patted LeBeau's shoulder as the two walked past one another. He gathered himself, then looked directly at Fullwood.

"The jury heard that my parents were disgraced Enemies of the People and somehow I was motivated by revenge. It made a nice story, but it was more of the same lies we've been fed for decades in the hopes that we won't start thinking for ourselves. Here's the truth: my dad, Michael Goodman Askin, was poisoned by the regime while he was in prison for something he didn't do. That used to be called a miscarriage of justice, if not murder. Before he died, he was depressed and told me all this struggle for freedom and justice was useless."

Dash could hear Polly choking up.

"I didn't believe it then, and I don't believe it now. When you give up your dream of a better world, you lose something as essential to human life as air and water. You lose your soul, and at the center of the soul sits hope, the ability to seek light in the darkness. Clary said it best. This is all bullshit. One day, we'll return to our senses. I have to believe that. One day, the fear that imprisons us all from one Boss to another will weaken and drift away. The hatred and intimidation will cease. The perversion of religion will end. We'll address our own failings instead of blaming others. We'll put Passivism and greed behind us. We'll set aside 'me' and take joy in 'us.' On that day, I'll stop fighting for my daughter because I won't fear for her future. I'm going to quote from a banned book by Thomas Paine. He said: 'I should suffer the misery of devils were I to make a whore of my soul by swearing allegiance to one whose character is that of a sottish, stupid, stubborn, worthless, brutish man.' You can put me away, Judge Fullwood, but you'll never get me to swear allegiance to any tyrant, father or son."

Fullwood knew Paine's words and knew the book. He could have stopped Dash, but he let it go.

The sentencing hearing lasted just twelve minutes. Without explanation or admonishment, Fullwood sentenced Dashiel Askin and Clary LeBeau to ten years in prison each. Wild Bill had told them right after the verdict that ten was the best they could hope for and that, in the random selection of Fullwood as the presiding judge, God was watching over them. Polly and Lily could visit Dash once a month at Upstream Penitentiary, Fullwood said. LeBeau would be sent to a prison in Kansas. There would be no time off for good behavior, but time would be added for recalcitrance.

Dash was in his blue jumpsuit, handcuffs, and ankle chains for the ride to Upstream Pen. He knew the route well. It was a concrete highway for a time, then turned toward the river, where lush trees and lawns spread from the bank between Victorians with wide porches and picket fences. Kids rode their bikes, and squirrels darted up trees. Boss Nation flags flew here and there, and Dash found himself sinking ever so gradually into a state of nothingness.

Upstream was a fine penitentiary, as prisons go, although it didn't seem to emphasize penitence in any way. There was no Halcitol. The food was poor, but so was the food at Thirteen. The guards were tolerable as long as you didn't antagonize them, but they weren't a bit friendly, like the attendants at the Sanctuary. Dash vowed to write to his friend Clary LeBeau in code that the censors wouldn't be able to decipher. The bed was awful, and his back began to suffer. He thought he might tolerate the winters but feared the summers would be brutal without sufficient air conditioning.

Not long after he arrived, Dash was jogging in the penitentiary's walled-in ball field when he ran into someone he knew. George Remington Huff looked thinner and a bit older, but he smiled broadly when he recognized Dash.

"I thought I might find you here," Huff said. "What a journey, huh?"

"Nothing like yours, I imagine," Dash replied. "Tell me what happened."

"Before or after I testified?"

"Both."

The two men walked the perimeter, hands in pockets, thrust into an uncommon camaraderie.

"Something just cracked when I went to see Hector Saletan. I should have seen it coming. I recorded it because that's what you do in the regime. Everybody does it. For protection, right? But when I got home after the shouting, I was pretty shaken. I was about to be fired, and it just hit me that this was all wrong. I don't mean getting fired. I mean the whole way the regime operates. I thought I believed in Prayer, Order, Security, and Shut-up-ism. I really did. Shut-up-ism did bother me, but I never listened to my instincts. I went with the crowd. I was ambitious. After I got home, I looked at the video I'd taken of Saletan. It just shocked me. I realized I had stopped thinking for myself, and that bothered me. I'd allowed him to treat me like dirt for terrible reasons."

"Are you married?"

"Yeah. One kid. Four years old."

"Sorry."

"Don't be. The marriage was already on the rocks. She's big into Bossism and loves that Junior is taking over. Can you imagine? She filed divorce papers immediately after I testified, and that was fine with me. It's my son I'm worried about. She's going to raise him to be a Passivist and a follower, I imagine. That's what kills me. I thought a long time about calling Abrams during the trial. He's a persuasive man. I wanted to give him the video anonymously, but he convinced me that testifying would have a huge impact."

"It did."

"Well, not enough to save you two. I don't regret it, though. The day after I testified, they charged me with theft of government property, unauthorized recording, and, guess what, seditious conspiracy. I got off on that last charge but not the others. The trial lasted just two days. So here I am. A convicted prosecutor. Two years in the pen if I behave. Four if I don't. Who knows what Boss Junior's gonna do."

"I don't think you want to be seen with me," Dash said.

"Not gonna happen, Mr. Askin. After my arrest, I felt whole for the first time in a long time. I realized how venomous everything had gotten inside the regime. I reacquainted myself with a set of beliefs that felt more like me. And those beliefs didn't include Bossism. When I was in jail, a friend brought me three short books stitched together and hidden inside another cover. He brought me 'Letter from Birmingham Jail' by a writer I didn't know named King. He brought me Thoreau's 'Civil Disobedience,' which I'd heard of because it was on the banned list. And he brought a collection of essays by the guy you quoted, Thomas Paine. His books are banned but you can look up his biography. Paine was tried for seditious libel in England. Reading those essays, it was the first time I really understood what Bossism destroyed. I mean the ideas it destroyed. It's such an easy thing to want a Boss running your life, right? It's comforting. Thinking for yourself is too hard for some people. They just know they're unhappy, and along comes a Boss who explains everything — he tells you how people are taking your job and your money, and he makes you think he's going to fix all of it. And you turn over everything, all your agency as a human being, to one obsessive man."

Dash told him: "During the trial, I looked at you and saw a soldier for Bossism blindly following orders."

"Well, that's what I was. I was floored when we realized you had somehow read the regime so accurately that your jokes, the Fuckings, turned out to be true."

"Divine intervention."

"But you don't even believe in God, do you?"

"Not really. I'm not an atheist, either."

"So what do you believe in, besides the need to end Bossism?"

"I guess what you've shown me today, George: the potential goodness of men. It gets harder to find as the years go by, but if you don't believe in the potential goodness of men, what is there?"

A month passed before Lily and Polly were allowed to visit. Dash worried most about his daughter. She seemed hesitant and awkward during their phone calls. But as soon as the two entered the prison visitor room, Dash saw that Lily had looked inside herself and decided to help cheer up her father. He also noticed that Lily stopped using 'Daddy' and addressed him as 'Dad.' It was Lily's idea, Polly told him. When she and Lily talked about it, Polly thought it was a great way to show Dash that, although she was grieving for him, it would be alright and he needn't worry.

The idea that Lily was taking confident steps toward adulthood lifted Dash's spirits more than anything that day.

Through the glass separating the family, Dash told them a little about prison life without dwelling on the loneliness and a lot about his state of mind, which he called 'healthy.'

"I've been writing," he revealed. "I'm going to try to write a memoir, even though I'm pretty sure no one in this country would be willing to publish it. Can I give you the first fifteen pages, Pol?"

"Can I read it?"

"Of course you can," he said. "But you should know it'll be raw at times. I don't think it dances around the hard truths."

"I'd have been surprised if it did," Polly told him.

Dash pushed a sheaf of neatly folded handwritten pages through the slot in the glass.

"I sort of need you to come back to pick up more."

"Oh, Dash. You know we'll be back every chance we get."

"I know. I just need to envision you walking into the visitor room. I'll have a smile on my face and so will you. It does get lonely in here."

Polly took out a tissue and wiped her eyes. She told Dash about the people she didn't know who were stopping her on the street and whispering things like: "Tell him to hold on" and "We're pulling for him" and "He took down The Boss, you know." And she told him how Agnes Jones had been sent to Sanctuary Thirteen and Izzy Andruzzi to Sanctuary Eight.

Polly also told Dash about Lily's grades in school, which were excellent, as usual, but she left out the bullying Lily had encountered after the verdict. And she didn't tell Dash about the billboards that went up on a few highways nearby, the ones with his likeness and LeBeau's, both standing in handcuffs, and the bold text "The Faces of Sedition." They were paid for by The League of Christian Voters.

Even as she assured Dash that everything at home was fine and was going to be fine, Dash couldn't imagine what Polly was going through.

"I believe in you, Dash, more than ever," she told him, placing the palm of her hand against the glass. He placed his hand on the other side in a mirror image.

Polly looked at Lily, who had practiced what she was going to say.

"Dad, I'm not afraid and neither is Mom."

"I know, sweetheart. Don't ever be afraid."

"Mom taught me a poem."

"She did?"

"It's long but I memorized the first four lines. I really like them."

"Can you recite them?"

"Okay." Lily paused, then lifted her eyes. "Let America be America again. Let it be the dream it used to be. Let it be the pioneer on the plain seeking a home where he himself is free."

"Langston Hughes," Dash said, nodding. "He's banned, but one day they'll revive his work. You know Mr. Abrams, Lil? He's back inside Sanctuary One. Would you like to visit him?"

"Yes. He was nice."

"You and Mom should go see him and tell him I'm fine. Go see Agnes Jones and tell her to keep her spirits up."

"We will," Lily said.

"At the trial, Mr. Abrams taught me a little Latin poem. It's just a phrase. It means, 'While I breathe, I hope.'"

Lily smiled. "We won't lose hope, Dad. I'm going to look for the light."

END

Acknowledgements

I am indebted to two astute readers of the early manuscript. Dr. Paul Bloom provided thoughtful, detailed suggestions on tone, plot, and character development. Nan Hayes employed her reliably keen eye to offer insight into ways to improve voice, structure, and pace. Her encouragement was also invaluable.